Wauconda A
801 N. Ma
Wauconda, IL 60084

AUG 2 8 2020

Howloween
Murder

Books by Laurien Berenson

A PEDIGREE TO DIE FOR
UNDERDOG
DOG EAT DOG
HAIR OF THE DOG
WATCHDOG
HUSH PUPPY
UNLEASHED
ONCE BITTEN
HOT DOG
BEST IN SHOW
JINGLE BELL BARK
RAINING CATS AND DOGS
CHOW DOWN
HOUNDED TO DEATH
DOGGIE DAY CARE MURDER
GONE WITH THE WOOF
DEATH OF A DOG WHISPERER
THE BARK BEFORE CHRISTMAS
LIVE AND LET GROWL
MURDER AT THE PUPPY FEST
WAGGING THROUGH THE SNOW
RUFF JUSTICE
BITE CLUB
HERE COMES SANTA PAWS
GAME OF DOG BONES
HOWLOWEEN MURDER

Published by Kensington Publishing Corporation

Howloween Murder

LAURIEN BERENSON

KENSINGTON BOOKS
www.kensingtonbooks.com

This book is a work of fiction. Names, characters, and incidents either are products of the author's imagination or are used fictitiously. Any resemblance to actual persons living or dead, or events, is entirely coincidental.

KENSINGTON BOOKS are published by

Kensington Publishing Corp.
119 West 40th Street
New York, NY 10018

Copyright © 2020 by Laurien Berenson

All rights reserved. No part of this book may be reproduced in any form or by any means without the prior written consent of the Publisher, excepting brief quotes used in reviews.

All Kensington titles, imprints and distributed lines are available at special quantity discounts for bulk purchases for sales promotion, premiums, fund-raising, educational or institutional use. Special book excerpts or customized printings can also be created to fit specific needs. For details, write or phone the office of the Kensington Special Sales Manager: Kensington Publishing Corp., 119 West 40th Street, New York, NY, 10018. Attn. Special Sales Department. Phone: 1-800-221-2647.

Kensington and the K logo Reg. U.S. Pat. & TM Off.

Library of Congress Control Number: 2020935635

ISBN-13: 978-1-4967-3057-2
ISBN-10: 1-4967-3057-7
First Kensington Hardcover Edition: September 2020

ISBN-13: 978-1-4967-3059-6 (ebook)
ISBN-10: 1-4967-3059-3 (ebook)

10 9 8 7 6 5 4 3 2 1

Printed in the United States of America

Howloween
Murder

Chapter One

"There's a ghost in the attic," Cheryl Feeney told me.

"No, there isn't," I replied firmly.

The Joshua Howard mansion, home to Connecticut private school Howard Academy, was one hundred years old, but there'd never been serious talk of a ghost before. Sure, sometimes kids played around with the idea, trying to scare one another. But a real ghost? That was new.

I had been the special needs tutor at Howard Academy for nearly a decade. If the mansion was haunted, surely I'd have heard about it before now.

On the other hand, Halloween was less than a week away. The upcoming holiday gave everyone at the school a chance to dress up in costumes and pull harmless pranks. It also pretty much guaranteed us a sugar rush. So maybe we were all feeling a little silly in anticipation.

Cheryl Feeney taught first grade and was new at HA this year. She was bright, and enthusiastic, and she loved working with children. In her twenties and fresh out of school herself, Cheryl took her responsibilities very seriously. She and I were putting together Friday's Halloween party, which was what had brought her to my classroom in the school's new wing.

Now, as Cheryl stood in front of my desk, she didn't look as though she was fooling around. Idly I wondered if she knew there was a smudge of dust across her cheek and a cobweb tangled in her blond ponytail.

"I know the mansion's an old building," I said. "But it doesn't have a ghost."

"It does," Cheryl insisted. "Up in the attic. I saw it just now. Come on, I'll show you."

"You'll show me?" Okay, that offer got me to my feet. "Like it's just standing there, waiting around to be seen?"

"I wouldn't say it's standing, exactly." Cheryl chewed on her lower lip. "More like floating. You know?"

I didn't, actually. But apparently I was about to find out. Despite the length of my tenure at the school, I'd never previously had a reason to visit the mansion's attic. So that would be a first too.

I snapped my fingers and Faith, my big black Standard Poodle, hopped up from her bed in the corner of the room. She was a beautiful dog, who stood nearly as high as my waist. A retired show champion, Faith wore her hair in the easy-to-maintain kennel trim, with a short blanket of dense curls covering her body and a plush pompon on the end of her tail. She came trotting eagerly across the room to join us. Whatever kind of adventure I had in mind, Faith was always ready to go.

Nine years old now, Faith was well into middle age. Her body had thickened in the middle, and she wasn't as energetic as she'd once been. The bond she and I shared had grown more meaningful over the years. Faith read my thoughts, supported my ideas, and sometimes understood me better than I understood myself.

That wasn't surprising, considering that she was a Poodle. The breed isn't just intelligent and playful, they're also naturally empathetic. Fortunately for the students of Howard Academy, I wasn't the only one who got to benefit from Faith's many good qualities.

HA was situated on a bluff overlooking downtown Greenwich, with Long Island Sound visible in the distance. The school's reputation was every bit as lofty as the prominent position of its real estate. Howard Academy counted senators, CEOs, and groundbreaking scientists among its distinguished alumni.

Our K–8 program offered a rigorous curriculum meant to give children the best possible start on the road to success. Not every child whose parents wanted them to receive a Howard Academy education was equipped to deal with that kind of pressure, however. That was where I came in.

It was my job to tutor students who were struggling—for whatever reason—to keep up. Sometimes their application to their studies needed my individual oversight. Some kids were having social or emotional problems. Occasionally they just needed a sympathetic ear.

No matter the issue that brought them to my classroom, kids were always delighted to find Faith waiting for them. Students accepted my tutoring, but they adored my Poodle. Over the years, she'd become Howard Academy's unofficial mascot.

Cheryl Feeney had only been at Howard Academy since the beginning of the fall semester. And since the first-grade homeroom was in the mansion, this was her first visit to my classroom. So I wasn't surprised that her eyes widened when Faith leapt to her feet.

I was surprised, however, when Cheryl shrieked, then jumped around behind me as Faith approached. The Poodle's tail was up over her back and wagging happily. Her lovely head tipped to one side, Faith appeared to be as confused by the woman's reaction as I was.

"Oh, my God!" Cheryl exhaled sharply. "What is

that? It's enormous! What's it doing here? Does it bite?"

"That's Faith." I held up my hand and the big Poodle stopped in front of me. "She's a Standard Poodle."

"No, n-no, n-no, she's not," Cheryl stuttered. She was still hiding behind me. Her ponytail swung back and forth as she shook her head vigorously. "Poodles are little itty-bitty things. They don't look like *that*."

"Some of them do," I told her. "She's very friendly. Would you like me to introduce you?"

"To *that*?"

"No, to *her*. Faith's a girl." A bitch, in dog parlance, but I didn't think it would help to tell Cheryl that. "She likes everybody."

"Not me. Dogs don't like me. They bite me."

"Faith doesn't bite."

"Sure. That's what you say now."

I turned to look at her over my shoulder. I found it mildly amusing that Cheryl was using me as a human shield. "There's no need to be afraid of her."

"I'm not afraid. I just don't like dogs anywhere near me. Like, ever."

I sighed. It looked as though Faith wasn't going to be coming with us to the mansion. I leaned down and scratched beneath the Poodle's chin. Her dark brown eyes stared into mine. Dammit, she knew what was coming.

"Sorry, sweetie," I said. "I guess you'll have to stay here. Go back to your bed and lie down, okay? I won't be gone long."

Faith's tail drooped. She sighed under her breath. Slowly she turned around and walked back to the cedar bed. If you think kids know how to make you feel guilty when you screw up, try having a Poodle.

Cheryl peered at Faith over my shoulder. "Why did she do that?"

"Do what?"

Her finger lifted in a wobbly point that was directed at Faith. "She went away."

"Because I asked her to."

"Yes, but she's a dog."

"An obedient dog."

I headed for the door. Cheryl quickly followed.

"And a smart one," I added. "Faith could probably help teach your first graders how to add."

As we left the room, Cheryl cast a furtive glance backward. Faith was back on her bed, just where she was supposed to be. "You're kidding, right?"

"Nope."

"Really?" Frowning, she looked back again. "Because that seems unlikely."

"So does your ghost," I pointed out. "And yet here we are, going to have a look."

"I know I saw *something*." Cheryl skipped around in front of me to lead the way. "The ghost is real."

Maybe. Strange things had been known to happen at Howard Academy before. And Halloween—the night when ghouls and goblins came out to play—was right around the corner. Maybe anything was possible this time of year.

Even a ghost in old Joshua Howard's attic.

Chapter
Two

Cheryl and I walked through the passageway that connected the school's new building to the mansion. I followed as she bypassed several classrooms and headed directly to the older building's soaring front hall. The large entryway smelled of lemon polish and fresh flowers. Its gleaming hardwood floor, crystal chandelier, and hand-rubbed antique furniture were part of a heritage that had been meticulously preserved through the years.

Twin portraits of the school's founders, siblings Joshua and Honoria Howard, stared down at us gravely from a side wall. The first time I'd seen the paintings, I'd stopped and stared in awe. Now I was more entertained by a pair of carved pumpkins someone had placed on a sideboard beneath them. The jack-o'-lanterns' somber expressions appeared to mirror those on the founders' faces.

I bit back a laugh and hoped I wasn't around when

our esteemed headmaster, Russell Hanover II, noticed that.

Cheryl was already skipping up one side of the hallway's split staircase. I hurried to catch up.

"I've never been up in the attic," I said. "But if it's as big as the basement, it must be huge. What were you doing up there anyway?"

Cheryl glanced back at me. "I thought I told you."

I considered briefly, then shook my head.

"You know, the Halloween party."

As the teacher with the least seniority, Cheryl had gotten roped into organizing this year's holiday party. Then Mr. Hanover had pointed out that since my tutoring schedule was light this semester, I might want to volunteer to help out.

I'd learned my first week at Howard Academy that when the headmaster made a suggestion, the only sensible response was to jump to comply. So I did. Which still didn't explain why we were on our way to the attic.

"All the props and decorations from previous holiday parties are in the storeroom next to the auditorium," I said. "You know that, right?"

"Sure. That was the first thing you told me."

"What was the second thing?" I asked.

She stopped on the second-story landing so abruptly, I nearly ran into her. "You said, 'Let's not try to reinvent the wheel.'"

"Good advice," I pointed out.

"Well, sure—if you've been teaching here for *years*." A smile softened Cheryl's words. "But I'm new. And I've been given a special assignment. So I really want to ace it. I know I was lucky to get this job at Howard Academy. I want Mr. Hanover to be impressed, and then he'll know he made the right decision to hire me."

I nodded. I could see that. Cheryl wasn't the only one who felt fortunate to be working at the school.

"And that meant checking out the attic?" I asked.

"Sure, why not? I figured it had to be filled with old stuff, and maybe some of it would be useful."

"And?"

"I was right about the old stuff. The whole place is a treasure trove of . . ." She stopped and winced slightly. "Well, to be perfectly honest . . . crap."

That made me laugh. "Crap *and* a ghost. This adventure is sounding better and better by the minute."

Tucked at the end of the upstairs hallway was a plain, unmarked door. I'd have expected it to be locked, but when Cheryl grasped the knob and turned it, the door swung open easily. It didn't even creak.

As I peered inside the opening, a blast of cold air hit me in the face. A narrow wooden staircase angled upward at a steep pitch. I could only see the first half-dozen steps. Everything above that was shrouded in darkness.

I turned to Cheryl and said, *"Really?"*

"Don't worry. There's a light switch."

She found it on the wall and flipped it on. It didn't help much.

"Have at it," I said, gesturing toward the dimly lit stairs. "I'll be right behind you."

Cheryl braced one hand against the wall as she began to climb. I quickly realized why. There was no banister to hold onto. I had to watch where I placed my feet. The stairs were narrow and coated with dust. They groaned as we stepped on them.

The air around us was chilly and still. When I took a breath, I could feel my heart beating in my chest. We hadn't even reached the attic yet, and already the place had me spooked.

No wonder Cheryl thought she'd seen a ghost up there. At this rate, I might see one too.

"Almost there," she said happily.

"Thank God," I muttered under my breath.

Cheryl reached the landing and moved aside so I could step up to join her. It was darker here than it had been on the stairway. When my eyes adjusted to the gloom, I saw a naked lightbulb hanging down from the ceiling on a twisted wire. Cheryl pulled the long string that dangled from it and the light turned on.

The sight in front of us was hardly worth the climb. The attic was a jumbled mess. It was piled to the rafters with decades' worth of odd items that previous denizens of the school hadn't wanted. And that no one in their right mind would want now.

In short, it was a cluttered mishmash of junk.

"Well," I said after a moment. "This is interesting."

Cheryl turned to me and grinned. "I know, right?"

The woman had entirely too much enthusiasm for her own good. "If you can find something up here to use for the Halloween party, you're a miracle worker," I said.

"Oh, I've pretty much given up on that. Once I started trying to sort through this mess, I realized it wasn't going to work." Cheryl headed toward a narrow aisle between two tall stacks of packing crates.

I brushed a cobweb out of the way and followed. "Then remind me again why we're here?"

"You said you wanted to see the ghost."

I nearly stopped in my tracks. Surely she didn't think this adventure had been my idea?

Suddenly Cheryl screamed. She jumped backward and stumbled into me. I grabbed her shoulders to steady her.

"Is it the ghost?" I asked eagerly. I didn't see a thing.

"No." Her voice quavered. "A mouse."

Oh. Bad luck.

Cheryl began walking again. "The ghost was over here," she said as the cramped passageway opened up in front of us.

I hopped over the spikes of an old bicycle wheel and looked in the direction she'd indicated. I still didn't see anything resembling a ghost. But maybe what I saw wasn't what mattered.

"Can you see it now?" I asked.

Cheryl looked at me as though I was daft. "No. Of course not." She paused, then frowned. "Can you?"

"No. But it's your ghost. I was hoping you'd be able to point it out."

"My ghost," Cheryl muttered under her breath. "As if anyone would want to have a ghost."

Dust rose from the floor as she crossed the open area in two quick strides. Cheryl shoved a battered bookcase out of the way, then abruptly went still. One of her hands slowly lifted, her finger beckoning me closer.

For some reason, silence seemed like a good idea. I tiptoed softly in her direction. As if I didn't want to scare the ghost away. Like that was a real possibility. If I wasn't trying to keep the noise down, I'd have smacked myself in the forehead.

I reached Cheryl's side and looked where she was now pointing. A flutter of white, backlit by the grimy window behind it, made my heart leap into my throat. Then I got hold of myself and looked again.

"That's not a ghost," I said. Loudly. Just in case it was a ghost and was entertaining thoughts about coming closer.

"Are you sure?" Cheryl squinted in the half-light.

"Absolutely." I figured one of us ought to sound like she knew what she was talking about.

"Then what is it?"

"I don't know." Now I was squinting too. "Let's go see."

Cheryl placed her hand against my back and gave me a firm nudge. "You first."

We both edged closer. I pushed an old steamer trunk to one side so we could pass. It knocked into something beside it and a pile of damask curtains slithered off a nearby shelf, raising another cloud of dust.

Cheryl coughed. I sneezed. And the apparition fluttered again.

"It's coming toward us!" she squealed.

"No, it's not." This time, I was actually sure.

There was just one large cardboard carton remaining between us and our quarry. I was near enough to see that the ghost wasn't spectral at all. In fact, it looked as though it was made of fabric.

The box was too heavy to move. I skirted around behind it. And found our ghost floating in the air, waiting for us.

"Cheryl, come and look," I said.

"No."

I glanced back. Cheryl had her eyes squeezed shut.

"It's not a ghost. It's a nightgown."

"A nightgown?" One eye opened. "Really?"

"Or maybe a slip, I can't tell. Come and see," I invited again. This time, she did.

The sheer gown before us was draped over a wire dressmaker's dummy. Tentatively Cheryl reached out a hand to finger its silky fabric, now rotted and yellow with age. When a gust of wind found its way through the cracked windowpane beside us, the slip lifted and fluttered in the breeze.

"Darn it," she said. "Now I just feel silly."

I was working hard to keep a straight face. "It was an honest mistake."

"Sure. If you're an idiot."

"You're not an idiot." I held up my hand, thumb and forefinger positioned slightly apart. "But maybe just a little gullible?"

"You think?"

Both of us laughed in relief. Then we made our way back downstairs, careful to turn off all the lights and close the attic door firmly behind us. We parted in the front hall at the foot of the staircase. Cheryl had a class to teach. I'd decided to take Faith for a run around the soccer field to make up for deserting her.

As I crossed the wide reception area, I glanced in the direction of Mr. Hanover's office. On our way past earlier, Harriet, the headmaster's secretary, had been at her customary post, behind her desk outside the office door. Then she'd been on the phone. Now she was free. I sketched her a quick wave.

Harriet didn't respond. Unusual for her, she didn't appear to be busy. Instead, her hands were folded together on top of her immaculately kept desk. Harriet was staring off into space.

My steps slowed. Something was wrong.

Harriet was a fixture at Howard Academy, a vital cog in the system that kept the institution running smoothly. She looked like everyone's favorite granny, but she had the tenacity of a terrier when it came to seeing to Mr. Hanover's needs.

Harriet's days started early and ended late. Her calendar was sacrosanct. She controlled access to the Big Man with equanimity and purposeful aplomb, treating everyone with the same consideration no matter their position in the school hierarchy.

No one seemed to know how long Harriet had worked at Howard Academy. She'd simply always been there. The students joked that Joshua Howard must have hired her himself.

What everyone did know was that the headmaster's assistant was steady and dependable. When all hell was breaking loose, Harriet could be counted on to be a center of stability. But now as I drew near her desk, I saw that her face was pale. And her fingers weren't just folded, they were clenched.

"Harriet?" A moment passed before she looked up at me. "What's the matter?"

"It's my neighbor, Ralph," she said softly. "He's dead."

"I'm so sorry," I replied. "Were you close?"

"We were friends. But that's not the worst part."

"Oh?" I stood beside her desk and waited for her to continue.

"The police think I killed him."

Chapter
Three

"There must be some mistake," I said.

I expected Harriet to agree. Instead, she just stared at me blankly. That was when I really began to worry.

I'd met Harriet on my first day at Howard Academy. Now she had to be past sixty, but she moved with a brisk agility that prompted others to take note. With a twenty-year gap between our ages, I wouldn't have characterized our relationship as close, exactly. But we were colleagues who respected each other's ability to take on a job and get it done well.

Over the years, I'd watched Harriet cope with a variety of trying situations. Not to mention handling the sometimes-trying headmaster himself. The woman was clever, competent, and utterly trustworthy.

The Harriet I knew wouldn't kill anyone. And if

she did, she'd be smart enough to hide the body somewhere that the police would never find it.

I glanced down at my watch and made a quick decision. I had half an hour before my next tutoring session was scheduled. Faith would have to forgo her walk, but this was more important. I grabbed a nearby chair and pulled it up close to Harriet's desk.

"Tell me what happened," I said quietly.

Harriet stiffened in her seat. Her gaze slid to Mr. Hanover's office door. "Not here!"

"Somewhere else, then." I stood up, ready to go.

She started to shake her head. But Harriet's face was still ashen. And her eyes were wide and troubled. I wasn't taking no for an answer.

"I'm sure you're entitled to a break." Even as I said that, I realized I wasn't sure. Harriet was *always* at her post. Or at least somewhere nearby. More than once, I'd wondered if she slept beneath her desk after the rest of us went home at night. "You must get a few minutes off occasionally, don't you?"

She considered briefly, then said in a low voice, "Mr. Hanover is working on the budget projections for next year. I placed the files on his desk earlier this morning. That should keep him busy for at least another hour."

"Perfect," I said. "Let's go."

"Where?" Harriet gazed around the hallway uncertainly.

Normally, when something went wrong, everyone turned to Harriet for guidance. She was always the most imperturbable person around. Now, without thinking about it, I'd expected her to take charge. My mistake. It looked like our next move was up to me.

"How about the rose salon?" I suggested.

The cozy room was just on the other side of the hall. Originally one of the mansion's several drawing rooms, it was now mainly used for private meetings. I knew it would be empty at this time of day. Rather than waiting for Harriet to agree, I simply took her arm and led her where I wanted her to go.

There was a quiet click as I closed the door behind us. A pair of leather armchairs sat facing each other in the small alcove formed by a multipaned bay window. Harriet took one seat. I sat down across from her.

Harriet sat up straight, her fingers grasping the chair's plump arms. I was happy to see that color was beginning to return to her cheeks.

"Take all the time you need," I said. "Start at the beginning."

Harriet nodded. She was ready. "You know those marshmallow puffs I make this time of year?"

Of course I knew Harriet's marshmallow puffs. Everyone at Howard Academy did. The homemade chocolate-and-marshmallow treats were a cherished school tradition. Attendees at the Halloween party couldn't get enough of them.

"Yes," I said. "They're delicious. Everybody loves them."

She started to smile at the compliment, then abruptly frowned instead. "That's the problem."

"What problem?"

"I don't just make them for the Halloween party. I also hand them out to trick-or-treaters in my neighborhood. My puffs are very popular."

"I'm sure they are." I sneaked a look at my watch. I'd told Harriet to take her time, but I hadn't expected our conversation to take such a roundabout route.

"Friends and neighbors always ask me for my recipe. But I never give it out." Harriet issued a small sigh. "My mother made the first marshmallow treats in her kitchen when I was just a child. Later, when I was grown, she handed down the recipe to me. Now I can't bear to part with it. All these years later, it still feels as if those treats are what keeps our connection alive."

"Obviously, it's very special to you," I said. Other

teachers had also tried to convince Harriet to share her recipe. Until now, I'd never realized why it remained such a closely guarded secret.

"That's it exactly," she agreed. "But I live on a nice street in Glenville and I'm friendly with my neighbors. I would hate for them to think poorly of me. So instead of giving out the recipe, I start baking early in October. I make lots of extra batches and hand them out to half the block."

"That's very kind of you." Idly I wondered if there was any way I could get my name on that list.

"Most people freeze the treats until Halloween. Then, like me, they give them to kids who come by." She smiled contentedly. "It makes our street a very popular place to trick-or-treat."

That wasn't surprising. If Harriet gave me a batch of marshmallow puffs, they wouldn't last until the holiday. I'd devour them all myself.

"That was my sister on the phone earlier."

"Oh?" Harriet's abrupt change of subject caught me by surprise. I hadn't known she had a sister.

"Her name is Bernadette, but I call her Bernie. She's two years younger than me, but people say we look like twins. I was the studious sister. Bernie was the vivacious one."

Harriet had always been a very direct person, but now she was stalling. I figured that meant we'd reached the part of the story she didn't want to talk about.

"Did she call to tell you that your neighbor had died?"

"That's right. The police were the ones who told Bernie about it. They came by the house to talk to her."

Finally we were getting somewhere.

"We'd heard several days ago that Ralph collapsed in his house," Harriet continued. "He was an older man, and not in good health. An ambulance came and took him away. When we didn't hear anything further, we thought he must be on the mend. But then the police showed up this morning."

"Why did they want to talk to your sister?"

"The detective told her that Ralph's death wasn't related to his ailments, like we'd thought. Instead it turned out that he'd been poisoned."

"Poisoned," I repeated softly.

"Cyanide," Harriet told me. "The police went to Ralph's house this morning to look for the source."

"Did they find it?"

"They did." Harriet paused and swallowed heavily, as if she couldn't believe what she was about to say. "The poison was in the marshmallow treats I'd given him."

"You didn't put it there," I said quickly.

"Of course I didn't. I liked Ralph just fine. I had no reason to want to harm him. But the police don't know that. All they know is that the cyanide was found in something I'd baked and personally delivered to the victim."

"But still . . ."

Harriet waited for me to continue. As if she thought I might have a good ending for my instinctive protest. Too bad, I didn't really.

"That doesn't make you guilty," I finished feebly.

"In the detectives' eyes, it does. Or at least it makes me their best suspect. Bernie said they're on their way here to talk to me."

That wasn't good at all. Mr. Hanover was very unhappy when Howard Academy found itself involved in police matters. The headmaster's first priority was to protect the school at all costs. Among other things, that meant shielding its reputation from scurrilous investigations or media coverage.

He was apt to become testy when the subject—or even the mere possibility—was raised. Ask me how I know.

"Wait a minute," I said as something occurred to me.

Harriet looked at me hopefully.

"Didn't you just tell me that your neighbors freeze their marshmallow treats until Halloween? So where would Ralph have gotten one to eat now?"

Her eager look faded. "That's not hard to figure out. I just distribute the puffs, I don't tell my neighbors what to do with them. He wouldn't be the first person to thaw some out and dig in early."

"Oh." So much for that bright idea.

"Oh?" Harriet's lips pursed. "I sit here and pour out my troubles, and that's all you have to say?"

She was right. That response was hardly helpful. I tried again. "What do you need me to do, Harriet? I'll help in any way I can."

"You're serious about that?"

"Of course."

Harriet rose to her feet. "Then come with me."

I followed her across the room. "Where are we going?"

Her hand rested briefly atop the antique crystal doorknob. "To see Mr. Hanover. The police are on their way. Before they get here, I'd better break the news to him that they're coming."

Dammit, she was right. But I would rather stick pins under my fingernails than deliver this kind of news to the headmaster. Maybe my offer of assistance had been a little hasty.

Without waiting to see if I was following, Harriet marched across the front hall with a determined stride. Telling her story had obviously restored her equilibrium. Too bad the coming encounter was about to eradicate mine. I hurried to catch up anyway.

"We know he's busy," I said when Harriet stood before the office door, hand poised to knock. "Maybe this isn't a good time."

She turned around and glared. "Don't be a ninny, Melanie. You know perfectly well it's now or never. You offered to help. Well right now, I could use a little moral support. Are you with me or not?"

The question shamed me right down to my toes. I'd found myself in trouble with Mr. Hanover on numerous occasions. No matter the infraction, Harriet had always been a quiet source of support. Of course I would stand beside her now.

"Let's go." I grabbed the knob and pushed the door to the headmaster's office open. Too late, I remembered that Harriet had intended to knock first. *Oops.*

Once a formal parlor, Russell Hanover's office was a spacious and imposing room, decorated with impeccable taste. A massive mahogany desk was the office's centerpiece. The headmaster was seated behind it.

He was a slender man, with a pale complexion and an austere manner. Mr. Hanover spoke several languages flawlessly and conducted himself with dignity in all of them. His Savile Row suits probably cost more than my car. Beyond the fact that his brown hair was thinning on the top, the only indication that the headmaster was well into middle age was the wire-framed reading glasses that were now perched low on his nose.

He looked up in surprise as Harriet and I came barging into his domain. Well, I was the one who barged. Behind me, Harriet's footsteps were so soft that they barely made a sound on the Aubusson carpet.

The headmaster pushed his glasses up into place and immediately stood. Of course he did. There were ladies present.

"Ms. Travis, I see you need to talk to me. Perhaps you would be so kind as to make an appointment with Harriet?"

Naturally he would assume that I was the one with a problem. That was the way our encounters usually worked.

"I'm afraid there isn't time for that," I said. "Harriet has something to tell you."

Mr. Hanover looked at his secretary curiously. "Now?"

I nodded as Harriet stepped up beside me.

"I apologize for the intrusion," she said.

"It's quite all right." He closed his computer and

shuffled his papers to one side. "I'm sure you wouldn't have interrupted if what you have to say wasn't important."

"The thing is"—Harriet twisted her hands together unhappily—"the police are on the way."

"*Here?*" Though he must have known the answer, the headmaster clearly hoped he was wrong.

"Yes, sir."

"I see. That does sound serious." Mr. Hanover's lips thinned. "And their upcoming visit is with regard to what, exactly?"

"It's all my fault," Harriet blurted out.

The headmaster turned to glare at me. As if he was sure I was the one in the wrong, and that I'd convinced his assistant to cover for me. "Please take a moment to compose yourself, Harriet. I'm sure that can't be true."

I had to concentrate on holding myself steady because what I really wanted to do was shrink back into the woodwork. Russell Hanover's glare was a fearsome weapon. This wasn't the first time I'd felt its weight, and the experience didn't improve with repetition. Even when I hadn't done anything wrong, the glare never failed to make me feel as though I must be guilty of *something*.

"I'm quite composed, sir," Harriet said. "You should

know that the police are coming to question me about the untimely death of my neighbor. I've just learned that Ralph died after eating one of my marshmallow puffs."

I nearly fell to the floor when Harriet confessed that to me earlier. Mr. Hanover was obviously made of sterner stuff. A small wince and a brief closing of his eyes were the only signs of his displeasure.

"You'd better sit down," he said to Harriet. "It appears we have much to discuss."

I noted that I hadn't also been asked to sit. Nevertheless, I had no intention of deserting Harriet now. She'd wanted me at her side, and that was where I meant to remain.

That is, until the headmaster asked his next question. It was directed toward his assistant. "The marshmallow puffs you made for our Halloween party, have you already delivered them to the school?"

"I . . . Yes, I have."

"And where are they now?"

Harriet's eyes widened. She realized what he wanted to know. Then suddenly I did too.

"I put them in the walk-in freezer in the kitchen," Harriet said quickly. "Eight full trays on the lower racks to the right."

Mr. Hanover's gaze returned to me. "I believe precautions are in order. We can't take the chance that our supply of marshmallow puffs might be contaminated too. While Harriet and I consider our options, would you be so kind as to retrieve those eight trays and bring them here to my office?"

"Yes, of course," I stammered.

"Go, Ms. Travis." The headmaster pointed at the door. "Go now and run quickly."

Chapter Four

The Joshua Howard mansion was a Victorian-era building, designed in the belief that servants would be the ones doing the running. Apparently, no one back then had cared about the fact that its hallways weren't arranged in a logical fashion. I raced flat out on the way to the kitchen. Even so, it took me three minutes to get there.

Betty Plimpton was Howard Academy's head of food services. She was in the back of the room, supervising the lunch preparations when I came skidding through the swinging door. Doubled over slightly, I paused to catch my breath. When I inhaled deeply, I realized that the room was scented with rosemary, lemon, and roasting chicken.

In other circumstances, I'd have stopped to appreciate that. Now there wasn't time. Instead I straightened and turned to face Mrs. Plimpton, who was coming to greet me with a smile.

"You must be hungry. Most teachers wait in the dining room for us to serve them. Lunch won't be ready for another hour, but I can probably find something for you to munch on in the meantime."

"No," I gasped. "I mean, no thank you. That's very nice of you. But I'm here for a different reason. I need to get something from your freezer. It's important."

"I'm happy to help." Despite her words, Mrs. Plimpton looked perplexed. "But I have no idea why you'd want to appropriate something from our food stores. There's nothing in the freezer except the things we use to prepare school meals."

"And eight trays of marshmallow puffs," I said. Now that I was standing still, it was easier to talk.

"You're right, I forgot about them. We're storing Harriet's famous treats until the Halloween party at the end of the week."

"Yes, I know. Harriet told me." It seemed better not to mention the context in which she'd shared that information. "She'd like me to retrieve them."

Mrs. Plimpton frowned. "You're sure about that? There are quite a few, several hundred at least. And it's still several days until the party. Once they're removed from the freezer . . ."

"They'll defrost and start to go stale," I finished for her. "I'm aware of that. But it can't be helped."

And it wouldn't matter anyway. After today's events, Harriet's marshmallow puffs wouldn't be on the menu.

Mrs. Plimpton hesitated. She studied me for a moment. Howard Academy was a small community. I knew she would at least have an idea who I was. But that didn't prevent her from doubting the validity of my odd request.

"This isn't some sort of practical joke, is it?"

"Definitely not."

"Well, then." She rubbed her hands together briskly as if absolving herself of responsibility. "Let's get started. It'll be a lot to transport. Eight very full trays, if I remember correctly. Depending on how far you're taking them, we'll need to get you a rolling cart?"

I ignored the implied question. There was no way I was going to announce that the marshmallow puffs were going to the headmaster's office. "That would be great. Thank you for your help."

Fifteen minutes later, I was back in the front hall, this time accompanied by a metal kitchen cart loaded down with frozen treats. The area was empty—that was no surprise. This time of morning, everyone was doing their jobs elsewhere, just like I should have been.

I'd left the door to Mr. Hanover's office open behind me. Now it was firmly shut. Through the mansion's wide front windows, I could see that a dark sedan was parked just outside. The police must have arrived.

I wondered what I should do next. One thing I didn't dare do was check my watch again. By now, Eddie Mackelroy, my eleven o'clock student, would be twiddling his thumbs in my classroom. And that was if I was lucky.

Eddie was an inveterate mischief-maker. If he'd devoted as much time to his studies as he did to devising pranks, he wouldn't have needed my tutoring. Right now, it was equally likely that he was out in the second-floor hallway with Faith, bouncing a ball off the wall for the big Poodle to catch.

In which case, all three of us would be in trouble.

I rolled the cart across the hardwood floor and parked it behind Harriet's desk. I supposed I could leave it there and run back to my classroom. The marshmallow puffs were frozen and enclosed in cling wrap. It was unlikely that a passerby would even recognize them, much less snitch one. So I could probably leave with a clear conscience.

But on the other hand, the police were here. That meant something really interesting was happening in Mr. Hanover's office. I cast a furtive glance around the area. There was still no one in sight, which meant that no one would know if I crept over and listened at the office door.

That had to be fate, right?

On a normal day, Harriet would have been the one to prevent such an egregious breach of etiquette. Today her chair was empty. If I tried hard enough, I could see the hand of fate in that development too.

I inched closer and rested my ear gently against a burnished oak panel. And heard nothing. I shut my eyes to concentrate and tried again. Still nothing. Like really nothing. Damn this old mansion with its solid fixtures. Now I just felt stupid. I took a step back and thought about walking away. Then I lifted my hand and knocked on the door instead.

"Come," the headmaster said from within.

I turned the knob, nudged the door open, and peeked inside the room. Mr. Hanover was standing in front of his desk. His arms were folded over his chest. Harriet, looking nervous, was seated at the edge of a straight-backed chair.

A tall, distinguished-looking black man was standing near the fireplace. I recognized him from our earlier encounters: Detective Raymond Young of the Greenwich Police Department.

Impatiently the headmaster waved me into the office. Detective Young glanced up as I entered. "Ms. Travis." He inclined his head slightly. "Why am I not surprised to see you here?"

"I'm sure I have no idea," I said primly.

Maybe someone else believed that. I know I didn't.

"We were just wrapping up here," Mr. Hanover informed me. "Did you secure the marshmallow puffs?"

"Yes, they're right outside."

Wrapping up? I thought. That was quick.

I shot Harriet a look. She ignored me. Her eyes were fastened on the detective, tracking him as he crossed the room. She looked as if she was afraid he might decide to turn around and talk to her again.

"Detective Young will be leaving now," the headmaster said. "He had some questions for Harriet, which I advised her not to answer until she'd secured the services of an attorney. Howard Academy will, of course, provide assistance and resources with regard to that undertaking."

"Of course," I murmured.

Howard Academy protected its own. And thank goodness for that. Mr. Hanover would make sure that Harriet was in good hands.

Young looked back and forth between the headmaster and me. "These marshmallow things that are outside . . . are they from the same batch that Ralph Penders ate?"

We all looked to Harriet for confirmation. She nodded.

"Then if you don't mind, I'd like to take them with me."

Nobody objected to that. Mr. Hanover had been concerned that the treats might fall into innocent hands. Removing them from the school grounds seemed the best way to ensure that didn't happen.

Harriet and Mr. Hanover remained in his office. So it was left to me to help Detective Young transfer the trays of puffs to the trunk of his car.

"That's a lot of marshmallow," he said as we stacked the last two flats on top of the others.

I gazed at the treats wistfully. "They wouldn't even have lasted an hour at our Halloween party. The kids love them. Actually, so do I. They're delicious."

Young shook his head as he slammed the trunk shut. "It seems Ralph Penders thought so too. He'd gobbled a bunch right down."

"What happened wasn't Harriet's fault," I said quickly. "Whatever you're thinking, she didn't do it. Harriet is innocent."

The detective's dark brown eyes looked steadily into mine. Previously I'd found him to be a fair man, one who considered all the evidence before making up his mind. But now I wondered whether this time— even this early in the case—he'd already settled on his main suspect.

"We'll have to see about that, Ms. Travis," he said soberly. "Won't we?"

When I finally got back to my classroom—half an hour late—both Eddie and Faith were missing. My heart dropped into my stomach at the sight of the empty room.

One person delinquent on my watch was bad enough. Two was beyond the pale. I could only hope that Eddie and Faith were together somewhere safe— and preferably not within sight of an authority who might be tempted to ask questions.

I was debating where to look first when I heard the sound of running feet. I popped my head out the classroom door and saw Eddie heading my way down the corridor. Long pink tongue lolling out of her mouth, Faith was dancing happily at his side. The two of them looked inordinately pleased with themselves.

"Yo, Ms. T! Where ya been?" Eddie chortled as they entered the room together.

Faith ignored me and went directly to her water bowl. Okay, maybe I deserved that. I had left her on her own for quite a while.

A stack of Eddie's books was piled on the round table. He slipped into a seat beside them and grabbed his notebook off the top. Faith sighed and flopped down on her bed. I stared at the two of them incredulously. Both looked entirely innocent, as if they'd never left their assigned spots.

AWOL? Who us?

Three could play that game, I decided. If they

weren't going to explain themselves, neither was I. I pulled out a chair and sat down across from Eddie.

"What are those words coming out of your mouth?" I asked. "Some kind of rapper lingo? You're a white boy whose mother is a pro golfer. You wear a necktie to school. Nobody's going to believe you grew up on the mean streets. You're just making yourself sound silly."

"Yes, ma'am." Eddie grinned. "Whatever you say." He gave his vowels a posh, country club roll. "Is this better, ma'am?"

I shook my head fondly. "You drive me crazy. You know that, right?"

"Not on purpose," Eddie replied. He didn't look even slightly chastened.

"Thank you for taking care of Faith for me."

"Hey, no prob . . . I mean, you're welcome. Faith's a great dog. She and I went for a little run outside, that's all."

"We only have five minutes left to work together, and midterms are right around the corner. How about if we schedule an extra tutoring session for to-morrow?"

"Sure, Ms. T." Eddie slammed his notebook shut. "You're the boss."

Eddie left when the bell rang and I spent the next hour catching up on work I'd missed earlier. Between Cheryl's ghost and Harriet's marshmallow puffs, it had been an unexpectedly eventful morning.

My job at Howard Academy runs from eight thirty a.m. until one p.m., five days a week. The previous school year, I'd picked up my younger son, Kevin, at his preschool on my way home. This fall, he'd graduated to kindergarten. Kev was now enrolled in a class at HA, and he and I commuted both ways together.

My older son, Davey, goes to high school in our neighboring town, Stamford. He rides the bus, which gives me one less thing to worry about on hectic mornings when I'm running late. Since our household also contains six dogs and a husband, Sam, whom I loved dearly—but just two bathrooms and a limited supply of hot water—it seems like nearly all our mornings are hectic.

A few minutes before one o'clock, Faith and I went to pick up Kevin. Classrooms for the younger students are in the rear of the mansion. Once again, I made my way across the passageway from the new building. This time, I didn't even glance toward the front hall.

Dismissal was in progress when we arrived. Kevin's teacher, Jill Wheeler, was supervising the distribution of her kids to various moms and caretakers. Kev saw us coming and came running. He ignored me and threw his arms around Faith's neck.

Jill just laughed. "Nobody pays any attention to me either when there's an animal around. Kevin's doing great. He's a pleasure to teach. I'm delighted to have him in my class."

I thanked her and herded child and Poodle out to the parking lot. Kev was a charmer, all right. He was a fair-haired, blue-eyed replica of his father, right down to his killer smile. Kevin had never met anyone he didn't like. His only attitude toward life was full speed ahead.

When we reached the Volvo, he was bouncing on the balls of his feet. "Happy Halloween!" he cried.

"Thank you," I replied. "But Halloween isn't until Saturday."

I knew that didn't matter. Kevin loved all holidays. He was already excited.

He threw his backpack on the floor of the car, then hopped up so I could buckle him into his booster seat. Faith jumped onto the backseat beside him. I got behind the wheel and we were good to go.

"Saturday is still four days away," Kev said as we coasted down the long driveway. He was counting on his fingers. "That's a long time."

"The Halloween party is closer," I told him. "Just three days. It's on Friday night."

"How come?"

"Because this year the holiday doesn't fall on a school day. Lucky you. It'll be like having two Halloweens."

Kev considered that. "Will I get twice as much candy?"

"Maybe." I wasn't new at the mom thing—so I knew better than to make any promises about that. "Have you given any more thought to your costume?"

Sam and I were planning to dress up for the party as Gomez and Morticia Addams. I'd known that for a month. But even though the holiday was just a few days away, Kevin was still considering his options. As the person who would be charged with pulling together his costume, I was just hoping that he'd settle on something that could be whipped up without much advance notice.

"A ghost!" he cried gleefully.

I groaned under my breath. I'd had my fill of ghosts today.

"What's the matter with that?" Kev asked from the backseat.

"Nothing," I said quickly. "I was just thinking you might want to be something more exciting. Like an astronaut."

Davey had been an astronaut once, so we already had the costume. With a few nips and tucks, it could easily be made ready for round two.

"A ghost," Kevin repeated.

It wasn't the worst choice, I realized. I could throw an old sheet over his head and call it a costume.

"Or maybe a software designer," Kev mused.

That was new. Software design was Sam's field. So I knew where that idea must have come from.

"That could work," I told him.

"What do software designers wear?"

"Anything they want." *Yes!*

Kevin frowned. He didn't like that answer at all.

For five minutes, we rode in silence. Kev was looking out the window. Then his gaze drifted downward to Faith, who was lying on the seat beside him with her head nestled between her front paws.

"I know!" Kev announced. "I'll dress up like a Poodle."

This time when I groaned, I made sure he didn't hear me.

Chapter
Five

Stamford is a thriving metropolis on the Connecticut coast in lower Fairfield County. On the south end of the city, beaches flank the Long Island Sound. In midtown, numerous restaurants, corporations, and malls call the business district home. There are residential pockets spread throughout the city, but land becomes more readily available to the north. Neighborhoods there are quiet and spacious.

My family lives on the other side of the Merritt Parkway in North Stamford. Our house is classic Colonial in style. It sits on two acres of land, much of which is securely fenced for our dogs. Faith is just one of five black Standard Poodles we own. All our Poodles are former show dogs and they're all interrelated. The sixth member of our canine crew is Bud—a small, spotted mutt my teenage son, Davey, and I brought home after he'd been abandoned by the side of the road.

Ours is a busy household. Sometimes it's hard to

make yourself heard above the din. A recent family project involved carving a half-dozen pumpkins to decorate the front of the house for Halloween. Though that had mostly gone well, I was pretty sure Bud had nabbed a stray pumpkin stem and hidden it under the couch.

Kevin and I spent much of the afternoon running errands. When we got home, Sam waved to us from the top of a tall ladder, where he was fixing a loose gutter. Davey stayed late at school for soccer practice, then caught a ride home with a friend. So it wasn't until dinnertime that we all had a chance to connect.

The dogs had been fed before we sat down to eat, but they were hanging around the kitchen anyway. The Poodles stayed because they were always happiest being wherever their people were. Bud remained because he was ever hopeful that a stray tidbit would fall from someone's fork and end up in his mouth. With meat loaf on the menu, and Kevin as the little dog's champion, it wasn't a vain hope.

Faith and her daughter, Eve, were lying down behind my chair. Our two male Poodles, Augie and Tar, were under the table between Sam and Davey. Older bitch, Raven, was curled up in the dog bed. Predictably, Bud was beneath Kevin's chair. At less than twenty pounds, he was able to fit into all sorts of places the bigger dogs couldn't go.

Since we'd just sat down, Kev's plate was still full. I

made a mental note to keep an eye on his food, in case it started disappearing too quickly.

"How was school today?" Sam asked me. He was wearing a faded blue chambray shirt, and its color matched his eyes. The shirt's cuffs were rolled back to reveal the dusting of blond hair on his forearms. He helped himself to string beans while he waited for me to answer.

The question sounded simple, but something in his voice made me suspicious. Sam had been scheduled to spend most of the day in his home office. So there should have been no way he could know about what had happened at Howard Academy.

"It was fine," I replied smoothly. All my fingers were visible above the table, so I crossed my legs beneath it. Surely that was close to the same thing? "Why do you ask?"

"Just curious." When he smiled, grooves bracketed the corners of his mouth. "Fine, you say?"

I scooped a dollop of mashed potatoes onto my plate and nodded. "You know how it is at HA. Same old, same old."

"Funny thing." Sam's tone remained casual. "That's not what I heard."

"Good one, Mom." Davey sputtered out a laugh. He was a good kid, but he was still a teenager. So he loved poking fun at his parents. "I think he caught you red-handed."

Maybe. Or maybe I could still brazen this out.

"Really?" I batted my eyelashes innocently. "What did you hear?"

"That the police were called to the school this morning. Beyond that, Peg was a little light on the details."

Of course he'd been talking to Aunt Peg. I should have known.

Aunt Peg was a relative by marriage, but that had never stopped her from insinuating herself into every aspect of my life. She was nosier and had more sources of information than the CIA. A year earlier, she'd hit her seventies at a dead run, and she had no patience for anyone who couldn't keep up. If there was trouble brewing anywhere in the vicinity, chances were Aunt Peg wanted to get in on it.

She was also a Howard Academy alumna. I knew Mr. Hanover would have made every effort to keep news of Harriet's difficulties under wraps. So how did Aunt Peg know about it already? She must have gotten a report virtually live. I wondered who her snitch was.

"There isn't much more than that to tell," I said.

Pointedly I let my gaze drift to Kev's place at the side of the table. His plate was looking suspiciously empty, but now I had bigger things to worry about. Fortunately, Sam got the message. We'd discuss the rest after the kids went to bed.

"Good," he replied. "I'm glad to hear that."

Davey smirked at me and rolled his eyes. I was half-tempted to kick him under the table, but I was afraid I'd hit a Poodle.

"Guess what?" Kevin cried. All eyes turned his way. "I'm going to be a Transformer for Halloween."

"Good choice," Davey approved. The two of them high-fived across the tabletop.

"Since when?" I wanted to know. That sounded like a hard costume to make.

"I just thought of it," Kev replied happily. "I'm finished with my dinner. Can I be excused?"

Sam frowned at Kevin's plate. "Did you eat all that food or did Bud?"

Kev just shrugged. He was already sliding down off his chair. "What's the difference as long as it's gone?"

Just what I needed, a five-year-old philosopher.

I wasn't surprised when my phone rang as soon as we were finished with dinner. As usual, Aunt Peg's timing was impeccable. I supposed it wasn't beyond the realm of possibility that she had a spy inside my house too. Where Aunt Peg was concerned, no idea was too outlandish to consider.

"Well?" she demanded as an opening salvo.

"Hello to you, too." I sat down on the couch and Faith jumped up to join me. I settled her warm body across my lap and curled my fingers into the plush hair on the back of her neck.

"It's Aunt Peg," I whispered.

"I know who I am!" she retorted.

"I was talking to Faith."

"Oh." Aunt Peg sounded slightly mollified. "Tell her I said hello."

There was a pause in the conversation while I relayed her message. Aunt Peg also lives with five Standard Poodles. They're all related to mine too. Be glad I didn't have to pass along felicitations from all of them.

I'd been caught skirting around the truth with Sam. So with Aunt Peg, I got straight to the point. "How much do you know?"

"Not nearly enough. Thank goodness I have a handy source at the scene."

"Who?" I asked.

Aunt Peg sighed. Then waited in silence long enough for me to get the point.

Belatedly, I did. She wasn't about to give up her secret mole. She was talking about me.

"Harriet's in trouble," I said.

There was a short delay while Aunt Peg worked to place the name. "Harriet is Russell's assistant, right? The woman who sits at the desk in the front hall?"

"You're thinking of the right person—but Harriet's responsibilities encompass much more than that. When it comes to the inner workings of Howard Academy, she's the woman with her finger on the pulse. She's the headmaster's eyes and ears, and probably his right hand as well. There's nothing that happens at HA that Harriet doesn't know about."

"Hmmm." I could tell Aunt Peg was smiling. Useful people were her favorite kind. "She sounds like a good woman to know. What kind of trouble is she in?"

I spent the next ten minutes outlining the situation. Faith raised her head and pricked her ears while I talked. She was listening avidly too.

"Harriet needs someone strong and capable on her side," Aunt Peg said when I was finished.

"Mr. Hanover's already on it. He's making arrangements to hire her an attorney."

"That's good. But I was thinking of a capable *woman*."

"You?"

"Don't be silly. I'm not acquainted with Harriet, and I don't work at the school. What possible use could I be? I'm volunteering you."

I had to admit, I'd seen that coming. When it came to poking around in other people's problems, Aunt Peg was always encouraging me to get involved. If she ever needed a change of career, she would make a superb puppeteer.

"Harriet's a very private person—" I began.

"Pffft!"

"I've seen her at school nearly every day for the

last ten years and I don't even know her last name," I pointed out.

"Oh pish. That doesn't mean anything. Have you ever *asked*?"

"Well, no."

"Then I suggest you remedy that. Posthaste. Private person or not, Harriet needs someone in her corner. I see no reason why that person shouldn't be you."

For a sneaky person, Aunt Peg could be remarkably unsubtle at times.

"This isn't about Harriet," I said. "You want me to figure out who killed Ralph Penders."

"Two birds, one slingshot," she replied. "And when you put your mind to it, you make a perfectly competent stone."

The fractured idiom made my head ache. I did, however, catch the implied insult. Perfectly competent indeed.

"I'll think about it," I told her.

"Think fast," Aunt Peg retorted. "For Harriet's sake. It sounds as though she needs answers quickly."

I disconnected the call and turned to Faith. "What do you think?"

The Standard Poodle woofed her reply.

"That sounds like a no to me," I said.

Faith's tail thumped up and down on the duvet. She was just happy to be part of the conversation.

"Maybe you meant yes?" I tried again.

Her tail thumped once more. It looked like a split decision.

Harriet probably didn't need my help, I realized. Chances were, Mr. Hanover already had everything under control. Still, it couldn't hurt to check in with her when I arrived at Howard Academy in the morning.

You know, just in case.

The following morning, I didn't have to go far to find Harriet. She was sitting in my classroom when Faith and I rolled in. And we were half an hour early.

I'd built in some extra time so I could cruise over to the front hall and see if Harriet was at her desk. Which she clearly wasn't. Because she was seated behind mine.

"You're sitting in my spot," I said.

Harriet looked up and smiled. She'd clearly caught *The Big Bang Theory* reference. "I'd imagine it has a nice cross breeze and sits at just the right angle for viewing the room." She stood up and walked around in front of the desk. "I brought Faith a biscuit. May I give it to her?"

"Of course."

She held out her hand and Faith politely slid the peanut butter biscuit off her palm.

At five foot six, I was average height, but I felt tall standing beside Harriet. Her pewter-gray hair was usually perfectly styled and sprayed, but today one side was crimped and flat. It looked as though she might have slept on it. Speaking of sleeping, Harriet didn't appear to have done much of that since the last time I'd seen her. There were circles as dark as bruises beneath her eyes.

"Is there something I can do for you?" I asked.

"I hope so. Because otherwise I'm going to lose my job."

"No, you're not." My answer was quick and resolute. Harriet couldn't lose her job at Howard Academy. The mere thought was inconceivable.

"I am." She sighed. "It's going to happen."

We both pulled out chairs at the table and sat down. Faith was still crunching. She walked over to her bed to finish her prize.

"Why?" I asked. "How? I thought Mr. Hanover was hiring you a lawyer."

"He is. But he also wants to put me on administrative leave. He thinks it's for the best."

"Best for the *school*, you mean."

Harriet nodded. "He said it was for my own good, but I know better. He's afraid I'll become an embarrassment to Howard Academy. This is his way of easing me out."

"No," I said. "You can't let him do that."

Her gaze lifted to mine. "I can't *afford* for him to do that. I love my job, Melanie, but I also need it. I refused to go."

"Good for you," I said roundly.

"I have to fight for my place here. I don't have a choice." Harriet's lips curved in a small smile. "Besides, it's not as if he could manage without me."

I smiled back at her. "*None* of us could manage without you."

"I'm glad you feel that way." She reached over and placed a hand on my arm. Her fingers were smooth and slender. "I know you have a reputation for solving people's problems. The only way I'm going to keep my job is if Ralph's murder gets solved quickly and quietly. And I want you to help me do it."

Chapter
Six

"Help you?" I repeated. I hadn't expected that. "Like we both work together?"

"Why not?" she asked. "I have a good brain on my shoulders. Plus, I bet I'm already acquainted with most of the suspects. That gives me a head start. What I don't have is spare time. I need someone to do the legwork."

"Spare time," I said faintly. It wasn't as if I had an abundance of that either.

"I thought we could make a deal."

"What kind of deal?" I stared at Harriet across the table. She was turning out to be full of surprises.

"I like Cheryl Feeney. She's a good kid. Good at her job too."

Kid. I almost laughed. Cheryl was in her midtwenties. "I agree."

Harriet nodded as if that was a given. "Here's what I'm proposing. I'll do your bit, working on the Halloween party with Cheryl. That will free you up to find out what went wrong with Ralph's marshmallow puffs."

Her idea had immediate appeal. For one thing, planning school events was the pits. The affairs always had too many moving parts, people who volunteered to help but never showed up, and work that didn't get done until the last minute. By which time, I had either stress hives or indigestion.

Plus, teaming up with Harriet would get Aunt Peg off my back. And a happy Aunt Peg was always preferable to the alternative.

"You're sure you want to take over the party?" I asked. "Cheryl and I still have a lot to do."

My question didn't faze Harriet at all. Instead she looked relieved. "I've thrown together dozens of events here at HA, some with hardly any advance warning. This shindig will be a piece of cake. I could knock it out with my eyes closed."

I wasn't about to argue with that logic. Especially since it aligned so neatly with my own self-interests. I was off the hook. Even better, I had nothing to feel guilty about.

"You've got a deal," I said before she could change her mind. "Do you want to shake on it?"

Harriet gazed at my outstretched hand. "Is that how you usually do business?"

"Umm . . . no." I pulled my hand back. "I just thought it wouldn't hurt to make things official."

"Like when you have real clients?"

That made me stop and think. "I don't have clients."

"Who are all those people you help, then?"

"I guess they're my friends." Harriet and I looked at each other for several seconds. Then I said, "Like you."

Harriet blinked slowly, then nodded in affirmation. This time, she was the one who held out her hand across the table.

Abruptly we both seemed to realize that our friendship had been building for years, without either one of us noticing it. Now the relationship was real. Our handshake ratified it.

"Good," she said firmly. "Now let me tell you my plan. After that, all you have to do is execute it."

All?

"The execution is the hard part," I commented.

"Don't worry, you'll do great. Like I told you yesterday, the marshmallow puffs I brought here, and the ones that ended up with Ralph, weren't the only batches I made. Not by a long shot. Some years, I bake more than a thousand of those things."

"You said you hand them out on Halloween and also give some to your neighbors, right?"

Harriet nodded.

"The police took the puffs we had here," I said. "Will they be gathering up the others too?"

"I highly doubt it."

"Why not?" That seemed like a no-brainer to me.

Harriet folded her arms over her chest. "Because I didn't tell them about the other batches."

"You . . . *What?*"

"Think about it, Melanie. I'm in enough trouble, as it is. The authorities are already looking at me sideways. My job here is hanging by a thread. On top of all that, there was no way I was going to subject half my neighborhood to a police search."

"But the people who have marshmallow puffs need to know—"

"Of course they do." Her breath escaped on a huff of annoyance. "And those stupid treats have to be grabbed back before the holiday gets here and people put them to use. But the retrieval process needs to be handled quietly. Like, you know, undercover. That's where you come in."

Harriet didn't know me as well as she thought she did. Doing things quietly had never been one of my strengths.

"Believe me, I've thought this through," she continued. "I'm busy here all day. You go home at one o'clock. That gives you plenty of extra time to go traipsing around my neighborhood. I'll give you the names and addresses you need, so you can get right to work."

Harriet made it sound so easy. I wasn't convinced for a minute.

"Your neighbors don't know me," I pointed out. "Maybe they won't even answer their doors."

"They will. It's a friendly block."

"They're friendly with you. You *live* there. Maybe you should call them in advance and tell them what's going on."

"No way." Harriet gave her head a definite shake. "Not happening. If you think I'm going to tell my neighbors *over the phone* that I was involved in Ralph's death—and that the marshmallow puffs sitting in their freezers might be filled with poison—you need to get your head on straight. News like that has to be delivered in person. And that will work out perfectly, because then you can pick up the puffs at the same time."

No wonder Harriet had wanted to switch jobs with me. Compared to walking around her neighborhood like an angel of doom, planning a Halloween party suddenly didn't seem like such a bad gig.

"Even if I start this afternoon, there's no way I can visit everyone today," I pointed out. "What if before I'm finished, someone else eats one of your puffs?"

Harriet stared at me across the table. Her expression

was grim. "Tell me something. Do you believe that I poisoned Ralph Penders?"

"No. Of course not."

"All right, then you can believe this too. I'm positive there was no cyanide in any of those marshmallow puffs when they left my house. I don't even know exactly what cyanide is, much less where to get it or how to go about using it. So unless two of my neighbors are in the unfortunate position of having someone wish them ill—and frankly, the very idea strains credibility—I'm certain that the remaining batches are fine. This is just a sensible precaution."

That was Harriet all over. The woman was nothing if not sensible.

"Besides," she said as she pushed back her chair and stood up, "this will give you the opportunity to get the lay of the land. And ask some questions. Isn't that how you usually operate?"

I opened my mouth to reply, but Harriet wasn't finished.

"I'm damned uncomfortable—pardon my French—being the only suspect the police have their eyes on. Go drum up some more leads. Give the police another direction to look in. You'll be doing us all a favor."

She gave Faith a three-fingered wave, then headed for the classroom door. "I'm glad that's settled. Now I need to get to work. I should be at my desk already. Mr. Hanover will be wondering what's keeping me."

Harriet had settled things to *her* satisfaction. But she hadn't given me a chance to agree or disagree with her plan. Possibly on purpose.

This wasn't the first time I'd seen Harriet riled up. She was like a mother hen, calmly and quietly looking after everyone in her nest—until someone disturbed one of her chicks. Then she turned into a Pit Bull.

Always before, her impassioned response had been in defense of another member of the Howard Academy family. Now she needed—and deserved—one of us to step up and do the same for her. I wondered if she was worried that I wouldn't be willing to take on the task.

There was no possibility of that. I was just hoping I wouldn't let her down.

"Harriet?"

She'd almost reached the door when I called after her. Harriet stopped and turned around. Her features were set, as if she'd steeled herself in case I was going to deliver bad news.

"What's your last name?" I asked.

Harriet relaxed then. Her shoulders shifted beneath her tailored suit. She gave me a small smile.

"It's about time you asked. It's Bloom. My sister and I are Harriet and Bernadette Bloom."

"I'm looking forward to getting to know you better," I said.

Her smile widened. "Me too."

By the end of my school day, Harriet had emailed me a list of the people to whom she'd delivered marshmallow puffs. There were six names in all, three belonging to couples. Harriet had also supplied her home address and cell phone number. There was a note at the bottom of the page indicating that she expected her sister to be at home this afternoon. Bernadette would be able to corroborate everything Harriet had told me.

In addition to that, she'd already spoken to Cheryl and everything was copacetic on the party front. Harriet was a wonder at getting things organized. I suspected she was also sending me the message that she'd done her part—and now it was time for me to do mine.

Glenville was a hamlet on the west side of Greenwich. Formerly a mill town, it bordered the Byram River. Housing was relatively affordable compared to the rest of Greenwich. Lots were modest in size and many homes were of an older vintage. Small, quiet neighborhoods abounded.

Glenville was in the opposite direction from my house in Stamford. Fortunately, Kev had a playdate that afternoon and his friend's mom was picking both boys up at school. That solved one problem. But I also had Faith to think about. It was cool enough outside for her to safely wait for me in the car. I just hated when I had to do that. Faith did too.

Harriet's address was on a side street lined with 1930s-era Cape Cod–style homes. Her house was painted white, with pine-green shutters, and had ivy growing up one wall. There was a jack-o'-lantern in a front window and a wreath decorated with Indian corn on the door.

A small sedan was parked in the narrow driveway. I left my Volvo at the curb beneath a maple tree; its vivid yellow- and orange-colored leaves would provide plenty of shade.

Faith looked at me balefully as I cracked the car's windows. She knew what was coming.

"I won't be long," I told her. "Promise."

It was a short walk up the driveway to the home's front door. It swung open as I approached. My first thought was that Bernadette Bloom didn't look anything like her sister.

Harriet was petite, her sister was several inches taller than me. Harriet dressed to blend into the background. Bernadette was wearing bright yellow pants with a figure-hugging sweater. A multicolored scarf was twined around her neck. Blond curls framed a face whose artful makeup was working hard to conceal her age.

Bernadette had a mug containing a hot beverage in one hand. She used the other to push the storm door open. "You must be Melanie. Harry said to expect you. Where's your Poodle? Don't tell me you left her in the car?"

"Umm . . . yes?" Faith had many admirers at Howard Academy, but I hadn't expected her fame to travel off-campus.

"What, are you kidding me?" Bernie braced the door with her foot and gestured with her free hand. "Go get her. Harry told me she's the biggest Poodle in the whole world. I want to see that. You'd better bring her inside. That is, if she can fit."

Bernadette laughed at her own joke as I went to fetch Faith. She stared at us from the doorway as we approached. "Harry wasn't kidding," she said, ushering us into the house. "That's some Poodle. Does she do any tricks?"

"A few," I admitted reluctantly. I didn't want to sidetrack our conversation. "But she doesn't like to show off."

"Performance anxiety, huh? I get that." Bernadette shrugged. "Too bad. I bet she'd look great in a tutu."

Even Faith looked nonplussed by that comment.

She felt it was beneath her dignity to wear clothing of any kind. She'd have been horrified if I tried to dress her up like a circus Poodle.

"You drink coffee, don't you? Everybody does. Let me pour you a cup." Bernadette was still talking nonstop. "I can add a little kicker to it, if you want. Maybe a splash of whiskey?"

"No." I gulped. "Thank you, but just coffee would be fine."

"Come on, follow me into the kitchen. It's the sunniest room in the house this time of year. We'll sit and talk in there. Cream and sugar?"

"Just milk, please."

I'd expected to be interviewing Harriet's sister, but I'd barely gotten in a word thus far. At this rate, I'd be lucky if she let me ask a single question.

The kitchen was small and tidy. It had been updated since the house was built—probably during the 1970s, judging by the fact that all the appliances were avocado green. They matched the specks in the linoleum floor. There was a wide window in one wall and the room was flooded with bright afternoon light.

I took a seat at a kitchen table that looked older than I was. Faith sat down beside me. Bernie filled an earthenware mug nearly to the brim and sloshed some milk on top. Then she set it down in front of me.

"How about Faith?" she asked. "Does she want a bowl of milk?"

"No, thank you. Faith doesn't need anything." And certainly not milk. My mug was steaming. I took a cautious sip and scalded the tip of my tongue.

Bernie sat down opposite me. "Harry's told me all about you. Like how you're good at solving mysteries and stuff like that. She said you're going to get to the bottom of things. Thank God for that, because someone has to do it."

I nodded. It didn't even slow her down.

"Ralph was an old man, but nobody wanted to see him die. All I can think is, this must be some kind of horrible mistake. The way I see it, Harry's in need of a miracle. And you're going to be it."

Chapter
Seven

Well, that set the bar pretty high.

No one had ever called me a miracle worker before—and with good reason. Miracles were way beyond my abilities. It occurred to me that maybe Bernadette had added a splash—or more—of whiskey to her own coffee.

"Go ahead," she said. "Harry told me you'd have questions. Ask me anything."

"I'd like to go over some of the details of the story. Harriet told me what she knew, but I also want to hear your version of events."

"I can start at the beginning," Bernadette offered.

"That would be great." I tried for another sip of coffee and burned my tongue again. You'd think I'd learn.

"Harry and I grew up right here in this house. Thank God we did, because we'd never be able to afford to buy it now. The neighborhood has changed a lot through the years, but it's still a great place to live."

She was going back to their childhood? That wasn't the beginning I'd had in mind. Faith and I exchanged a glance. We were probably thinking the same thing. We were going to be here awhile.

"Harry is older than me," Bernadette continued. "You can probably tell that by looking at us."

Not really. But a nod seemed called for, so I obliged her.

She smiled happily. "There's not as much of an age difference as you might think. Just two years. Harry's the one with the brains. She went to college, and everything. She got married for the first time right after she graduated."

"The first time?" I repeated. I'd never previously given Harriet's love life any thought. But if I had, I wouldn't have imagined multiple marriages.

"Yes, she tried it three times in all. If you ask me, Harry just couldn't figure out how to settle down."

This was a whole different side to Harriet than the one I knew. It was also one I'd have never envisioned. Harriet always seemed to be the most settled person around. I winced at a sudden thought. If I was wrong about that, what else might I be wrong about?

"I was married just once, but I made it stick," Bernadette told me. "Seth and I lived together here in this house until he passed away ten years ago."

"I'm sorry," I said.

"Thank you. Seth was a good man. But when your time comes, there's nothing you can do about it. Harry was living over in Cos Cob back then. She'd already kicked Nate—he was number three—to the curb. At that point, it seemed silly for both of us to be rattling around separate houses on our own. So I set out the welcome mat and she moved in."

"It sounds like that was a good idea," I said.

Bernadette shrugged. "Some days better than others, but mostly we get along fine. Now where was I?"

"Perhaps we could skip forward to the day your neighbor, Ralph Penders, died?" I suggested.

"Oh yeah, Ralph. He was a nice guy. If he was poisoned, like the police said, he sure didn't deserve that."

"Is his house right next door?"

"No, it's down a couple from here. But that didn't make any difference to Harry. She handed out those marshmallow puffs to anyone who wanted them. She called it being neighborly." Bernadette snorted under her breath. "I don't even want to know what the neighbors are going to think about that now."

"I'm sure they'll feel the same way you and I do," I said. "That what happened couldn't have been Harriet's fault."

"I hope so." Bernadette didn't sound convinced.

"How did you find out about Ralph's death?"

"It was the two policemen that told me. Pounded on the door yesterday morning when I was still running around in my nightgown. They nearly scared the bejesus out of me. After I let them in, I had to race upstairs and put on some clothes."

"Why did they come here?" I asked curiously. "What made them think you would know anything about Ralph's death?"

"They didn't. Leastways not at first. They were just walking up and down the whole street, talking to anyone who was home. This is a pretty close neighborhood. So when Ralph collapsed a couple of days ago, we all knew about it."

She paused for a gulp of coffee. "The dying part, though. That came as a surprise. The two policemen told me about that. They asked if I'd seen anything suspicious happening around here recently. I told them, of course not. What kind of a place did they think this was?"

"Did they tell you how Ralph had died?"

"No, that was the funny thing." Bernadette frowned, thinking back. "They didn't tell me much of anything at all. They just kept asking questions. The kind of questions that I didn't have any answers to. But the two of them had interrupted my morning routine. And I hadn't had my coffee yet. So I went into the kitchen to make some."

"By yourself?"

"One of the officers came in here with me. Like I needed an escort or something. I mean, what was the man thinking? It's not like I was going to go running out the back door before I even had my makeup on." She chuckled at the thought. "So he was standing there when I opened the refrigerator to get out the milk. I wasn't paying any attention to him until he glanced inside and jumped back. I mean, he *really* jumped."

Bernadette hopped from her chair to demonstrate. Faith and I both watched in amazement as she leapt up in the air. This conversation was turning out to be all kinds of entertaining.

"He ran out of the room, then right away he came back with the other cop. The two of them started going nuts because Harry and I had marshmallow puffs inside our fridge. That was the first inkling I got that maybe something was wrong."

Maybe something was wrong? If I ever had a policeman jumping up and down in my kitchen, I would know right away that something was wrong.

My coffee had cooled enough to be drinkable and I took a grateful sip. I needed a good jolt of caffeine to keep up. "What happened next?"

Bernadette walked over to the coffee machine on the counter and topped off her mug. "One of the officers asked where I'd gotten the puffs from. I thought maybe he wanted to try one, you know?"

I did know. The treats looked every bit as good as they tasted.

"He said, 'No siree, ma'am.' Then he asked where they came from and what they were doing in my refrigerator. So I told him all about Harriet and her famous marshmallow puffs, and how she baked plenty to hand out around Halloween because everybody loved them so much."

The steady stream of words came to an abrupt stop. Bernadette inhaled a deep breath. "That's when the officer told me that when Ralph collapsed, he'd been eating one of Harriet's marshmallow treats. And that later on, when he died in the hospital, they discovered he'd been poisoned."

"It must have come as a huge shock to you."

She didn't speak. Instead, she just nodded.

"That's when you called your sister and told her the police were on their way to Howard Academy?"

Bernadette sniffled. She looked as though she was on the verge of tears. "Well, first I went and put on my makeup, because at that point, who knew who else might come barging into my house? *Then* I called Harry to let her know what was happening."

There was a light knock on the back door. Almost immediately it was drawn open. Startled, Faith jumped to her feet. I reached out a hand to steady her as a man came striding into the kitchen.

He was probably in his late forties, but his full head of dark hair—bangs falling forward over his eyes—gave him a boyish look. He was wearing a cashmere sweater with pressed jeans, and his loafers had recently been shined. His gaze went immediately to Bernadette.

"Hey, babe, I hope . . . Oh!" He noticed Faith and me, and stopped in his tracks. "Sorry to interrupt. I didn't know you had company."

"No problem. Come on in." Bernadette met the man in the middle of the room. She rested her hands on his shoulders as he leaned down to kiss her cheek. "This is Melanie. Harriet sent her to see if she can figure out how the hell Ralph died from eating marshmallow puffs. Melanie, this is my boyfriend, Hugh Grainger. He'll be happy to answer your questions too."

"You don't look like a policewoman," Hugh said with a smile. "And that definitely doesn't look like a police dog."

"I'm not with the police," I told him. "I'm just a friend, trying to help out."

He was still staring at Faith. "Does she help too?"

"Sometimes, in her own way. She's a Standard Poodle. Her name is Faith."

"Pretty girl." Hugh hunkered down in front of her. He held out his hand. "Do you shake?"

Faith sniffed his fingers politely.

"Shake?" When he made the request a second time, this time more forcefully, I knew what was coming.

Faith responded to the command in the way that show Poodles are trained to do. She shook. The motion started at her nose, with her feathered ears flying around her head. Then her body rolled from side to side. The spiraling movement ended at the tip of her pomponned tail.

Hugh stumbled back in surprise. That caused him to lose his balance and tip over. He ended up sitting on the floor.

Bernadette burst out laughing. I had to admit, it was pretty comical.

Hugh quickly scrambled to his feet. "What the hell was that?"

"You asked her to shake," I said. "So she did."

He wasn't amused. Taking a pratfall in front of Bernadette had injured his pride. "Is that supposed to be a joke? Because it's not very funny. I was just trying to be friendly."

I reached down and pat Faith so she'd know not to take his irate tone personally. "She was trying to be friendly too. Faith used to be a show dog. Poodles compete with a big coat of hair that gets scissored into shape. It's best if the dog shakes out first so the hair settles naturally into place. So Poodles learn to shake on command. And you gave her the command."

"No, I didn't." Hugh was still grumpy. "I was asking her to give me her paw. That's what she was supposed to do."

"I'm guessing you've never trained a dog," I said.

Hugh walked over to the counter and poured himself a cup of coffee. He was, I noted, very much at home in the Bloom sisters' kitchen. "Actually, I don't know much about dogs at all. It's probably my fault for trying to engage with her when I didn't know what I was doing."

Hugh picked up his mug and joined us at the table. "Sorry about the mixed signals," he said to Faith. "I guess you're a good dog, even if you did make me look foolish."

"Don't be silly," Bernadette said. "You could never look foolish."

Their gazes met across the table. For a moment, it looked as though he might lean over and kiss her again. Then Hugh seemed to remember that Faith and I were watching. He settled back in his seat.

"So you're here to ask questions about what happened to Ralph," he said. "How can I help?"

"Did you know Mr. Penders?" I asked.

"Not really. I'd seen him around the neighborhood a time or two, when I was here visiting Bernadette. He wasn't a friendly type of guy. We never had a conversation or anything. He had this way of standing there and looking right through you. I found it pretty unnerving."

"That wasn't Ralph's fault," Bernadette said quickly. "The poor man had dementia. It had been growing worse too. Ralph had good days and bad ones. Just like my family, he'd lived in this neighborhood for years. Even so, sometimes when he went out walking, he'd lose his way or forget where he was. Then one of the neighbors would have to go out and steer him back home. He never meant anybody any harm."

"Do you have any idea why someone would have wanted to poison him?" I asked.

"No," Bernadette replied firmly. "None whatso-ever."

Hugh shook his head too. "It's terrible to have something like that happen in a place where you should be able to feel safe. Ever since the police were here, Bernie's been on edge just thinking about it. That's why I stopped by today. I want my sweetie to know that I'm keeping a close eye on her."

The two of them reached across the table to twine their hands together. When Hugh squeezed Bernadette's fingers, a blush rose on her cheeks. Her lashes fluttered and Hugh smirked. Despite their ages, the pair looked like a couple of teenagers experiencing their first love.

It was definitely time for Faith and me to go.

"I'm glad you have someone looking out for you," I told Bernadette as I rose to my feet. "And Harriet too."

"Sure, Harriet too." Hugh's reply was perfunctory. He was barely listening to me.

Faith and I left the kitchen and let ourselves out the front door. I wondered how long it took them to notice that we were gone.

Chapter
Eight

I walked out to the sidewalk and looked up and down both sides of the street. All the houses were on small lots. The entire neighborhood was within easy walking distance. Assuming the people on Harriet's list were home, I should have time to talk to several of them.

Faith merely sighed when I took her back to the Volvo and locked her inside. She turned a small circle on the backseat and lay down, but not before giving me that look. You know the one. Without saying a single word, the big Poodle was able to clearly convey her disappointment in my dog-care skills.

I couldn't help it, I had work to do.

The name at the top of Harriet's list belonged to Trixie Dent. According to the number on the mailbox, her house was right next door. The sight of her front yard made me smile. Trixie had gone all out on her Halloween decorations.

On one side of the small lawn was a straw-stuffed scarecrow, its lower limbs resting on a row of pumpkins. Near the house, two life-size skeletons peeped out from behind the trunk of a sturdy tree. A cardboard cutout of a witch riding a broomstick was affixed to the front door.

The sidewalk between the two homes was covered with a blanket of autumn leaves. As they crunched beneath my feet, the sound abruptly transported me back to my childhood. My younger brother and I used to spend all day raking fallen leaves, only to undo our hard work by jumping in the pile and scattering them again.

Now it occurred to me that I hadn't raked even a single leaf in years. Not since Davey was little. And Kevin had never taken part in that autumn tradition. Suddenly that seemed like a shame.

People grew up. They got busy. Lives evolved. Sam was a man who loved his gadgets. He took care of our leaves with his blower. That was progress—but sadly, it felt like we'd lost something too.

I knocked on Trixie's door twice, but there was no answer. Midafternoon she could be anywhere. I made a note to try again tomorrow. Hopefully, the marshmallow puffs Harriet had given Trixie were still sitting, safely uneaten, in her freezer.

The next person on Harriet's list lived across the street. John Vidal wasn't into holiday decorations, but his front walk was neatly swept and his small yard was bordered by a flower bed with precise brick edging. Even better, a car was parked in his driveway. I hoped that meant I'd have more success here.

The man who opened the door in response to my knock had narrow shoulders and hips, and was as skinny as a sight hound. His T-shirt was tucked into jeans that rode low on his hips, and he was wearing flip-flops. In October. He barely looked old enough to drive, much less own his own home.

"Hi," I said brightly. "I'm looking for John Vidal."

"That's me."

"Oh, umm . . . okay." I'd assumed I was looking at John Vidal's son.

He crossed his arms over his chest and leaned sideways against the door frame. "Something wrong with that?"

"No. I was just expecting someone older."

He pondered that briefly. "How come?"

Good question.

"You look like you should be in school," I said honestly.

John Vidal shook his head. He seemed to be enjoying himself. "Nope. I'm done with school."

"Work?"

"My job's remote. I work from home, at least when I'm here. When I'm not, I work from somewhere else. I can make a computer do things most people can't even conceive of."

"I'll bet," I muttered. Technology wasn't my forte. A first grader could probably outprogram me.

"So, are you selling something?" he asked. "Cookies? Magazine subscriptions? Bibles?"

"I'm not selling anything. I'm a friend of Harriet Bloom's. I was hoping you'd have a few minutes to talk to me?"

He looked down at his watch. Not only wasn't it a smartwatch, it was analog, not digital. John Vidal was one surprise after another. "I guess I can spare five minutes. Unless what you have to say turns out to be interesting."

"Then what?" I asked as he stepped back from the doorway and I followed him inside.

He shrugged. "Then I might give you ten."

Bernadette had offered me coffee. John just waved vaguely in the direction of a couch, which was pushed up against a wall. When I sat down, he remained standing. His arms were still crossed. He already looked bored. I figured I'd better start with something good. Otherwise I might find myself back outside in a hurry.

"Harriet Bloom didn't kill Ralph Penders."

"Whoa!" That got John's attention in a hurry. "Who said she did? I thought the old guy just collapsed in his home. Didn't he die in a hospital?"

"That's right. But it turns out that he was poisoned. He died after eating one of Harriet's marshmallow puffs."

"No way!" He was grinning now. "Like for real?"

"Yes, for real. And it's not funny."

"Obviously not for Ms. Bloom," he said. "But for me? Sure. Let's just say, that news brightens up an otherwise mundane day."

"I didn't come here to entertain you," I snapped.

"Well, how would I know that? I'm still waiting to find out what you're doing in my house. So far, you haven't given me a clue."

He had a point.

"For starters, I need to retrieve the marshmallow puffs that Harriet gave you."

"Whoa," John said again. It was obviously his exclamation of choice. "Like they might be poisoned too?"

"Probably not," I told him. "This is more of a precautionary measure."

"Good thing. Because I ate half a dozen before I chucked the rest in the freezer to save for Halloween."

"You already ate some?" I stared at him in shock.

"Of course I did. Have you ever tasted those things? They're wicked good. If you ask me, they're wasted on trick-or-treaters."

I stood up and peered at him closely. The guy could stand to gain some weight, but other than that he looked healthy enough. "How long ago did you eat them?"

"I dunno. Three days ago? Maybe more?" He paused and frowned. "What do you think—would I already be dead if mine were poisoned too?"

"I'm not sure," I said. "I don't know much about cyanide."

"I can fix that." There was a computer on a nearby desk. John opened it and leaned down to hover over the keyboard. His fingers typed madly for a minute; then he squinted at the results.

"Yup," he said. "It's a fast-acting poison. If I was going to keel over, I'd have already done it."

"Good to know." I nodded. "I'm glad you're not going to die."

"Me too." John didn't seem unduly upset about his possible close call. "Now that we've gotten that out of the way, what else can I do for you?"

"Someone killed your neighbor," I said. "Did you know Ralph Penders?"

He stared at me. "What's it to you?"

"I'm trying to help Harriet. Like I said, she's my friend. We work together at Howard Academy."

John grimaced slightly when I said the school's name.

"What?"

"Nothing." He folded his skinny arms over his

chest again. Anyone could recognize that sign of resistance. "Go on."

"Not until you tell me what's the matter."

"It's no big deal. Howard Academy isn't my favorite place."

"How come?"

He shrugged.

I waited. I was a teacher. I could play this game all day.

"Did you go to HA?" I asked after a pause.

"No way."

"Do you know people who went there?"

"How would that happen if I didn't go to school there myself?" Now he sounded defensive. That pointed me in the right direction.

"Did you want to attend school at Howard Academy?"

John shrugged again. He was a man with a limited repertoire of gestures. "I didn't care. But my parents wanted me to go there. They thought the school would put me on some path to success later in life."

His parents weren't wrong, I thought. It was what we at Howard Academy strived to do. "What happened?"

"Nothing. I went to Glenville Elementary instead."

"How come?"

"Lady, you ask a lot of nosey questions."

"Yes," I replied mildly. I sat back down and made

myself comfortable. So he'd know I wasn't going anywhere until I got some answers.

John eyed my new position. His gaze narrowed. He'd gotten the message. "I needed a scholarship, okay? And I didn't get one."

"I'm sorry," I said.

"Don't be. Not going to Howard Academy didn't stop me from getting into MIT when I was sixteen. And graduating before I turned twenty."

I was impressed. As I was sure I was meant to be.

"Well done," I said. "Missing out on you was clearly Howard Academy's loss. And their mistake. It sounds as though you would have been an exemplary student."

Unexpectedly, John laughed. "I wouldn't say that. Not even close. Look, your time's running out. I offered you five minutes and we've already blown through that."

"You offered me ten if I was interesting," I pointed out. "Making you reconsider your own mortality for a minute or two probably qualifies."

"Fair enough," he conceded. "But you're still using up my day. Can we get to the point?"

"Sure. Back to Ralph Penders. How well did you know him?"

"Hardly at all, really. I mean, yes, he was a neighbor. But it's not like we had anything in common, you know?"

I nodded.

"Sometimes when it snowed in the winter, I'd go over and shovel his walk. He was an old guy, but he liked to wander around some. Ralph was healthy enough physically, but he could be kind of confused upstairs." John pointed to his head, in case I hadn't understood what he meant.

"Do you know any reason why someone would have wanted to kill him?"

"Nope. None." His reply was definite. "Ralph was harmless. He didn't look like he could hurt a fly."

I stood up to leave. "Would you get your marshmallow puffs for me so I can return them to Harriet?"

"I don't think so," John replied, but he was smiling.

"What if they're tainted?" I asked. "Harriet's just trying to ensure that no one else gets hurt."

"I thought we covered that," he said as he walked me to the door. "If I was going to die, it would have already happened. So why give up hours of eating pleasure on the off chance . . ."

"That you got lucky with the first few?"

"Something like that. Besides"—he grinned—"I like living dangerously."

In his world, that probably meant playing video games with gun battles and explosions.

"You can keep the marshmallow puffs on one condition," I said.

"What's that?"

"You know the risk you're taking, but other people don't. Promise me that you won't give any of those treats away, especially not to children who come to your house on Halloween."

John laid his hand solemnly over his heart. "I promise."

He pointed me in the direction of Bill and Becky Gruber's house—the next names on my list—and sent me on my way. There weren't any cars parked in the Grubers' driveway, but a woman opened the door before the melodious chimes of her doorbell had even finished ringing. She was dressed in a shapeless flowered garment that looked like a muumuu, and her face was pinched in a scowl. Judging by the deep creases in her cheeks, I figured it was probably a habitual expression.

Becky Gruber, I presumed. She stared at me suspiciously through the storm door, which was still closed between us, and said, "Yes?"

"I'm a friend of Harriet Bloom's," I told her. "Can we talk for a minute?"

"About what?"

"The marshmallow puffs she gave you."

"What about them?"

"Maybe I could come inside?"

"Why?"

It was chilly standing on the front step and I had to

yell to make myself heard through the glass door. I thought that was reason enough, but apparently not.

"Because I have some information that you're going to want to hear."

Becky shifted her weight from one slipper-clad foot to the other. She looked like she could stand there all day. A television was on in the living room behind her. Apparently I'd interrupted her soap opera.

"Why should I believe you?" she demanded. "How do I know this isn't a trick?"

I didn't really have an answer for that. At that point, I was sorely tempted to give up. Then I thought about the possibility that her marshmallow puffs might be contaminated—and the promise I'd made to Harriet to get them all back—and decided to give it one more try.

"Your neighbor, Harriet, is in big trouble," I said. "I need to talk to you about it."

The door rattled as Becky shoved it open. "Well, why didn't you say so in the first place?"

Chapter Nine

A blast of warm air enveloped me as I stepped into the living room. "You must be Becky Gruber," I said. "I'm Melanie Travis."

The woman ignored my greeting. She was looking around the room for something. After a few seconds, she found it: the remote control for the television. She didn't turn the TV off, but she did mute the sound. I supposed that was better than nothing.

"Is your husband, Bill, at home?" I asked brightly. "I'd like to speak with him too."

"He's at work." Becky rolled her eyes as if I should have known. "Whatever you have to say about Harriet, you can tell me."

She glanced back at the TV screen, where two characters were kissing. I could guess what she was thinking. Whatever I had to say had better be good, because I was making her miss her soap.

"It's about Ralph Penders's death."

A smile twitched briefly around the corners of Becky's thin lips. Now she was interested. She gestured toward a pair of squat, upholstered chairs. "Have a seat. Did Harriet do it?"

I perched on the edge of a plump cushion that felt like it wanted to swallow me whole. "No."

Becky peered at me closely. "You sure?"

"Pretty sure. Why? Do you think she did it?"

"Always a chance. That Harriet, she's smart. She could pull something like that off, and no one would be the wiser."

I agreed with Becky about that. Not that I had any intention of saying so out loud.

"What reason would Harriet have had for wanting your neighbor dead?" I asked instead.

"The same one we all had, I guess."

I tried not to look too curious. "What's that?"

"The man's a nuisance, has been for years. He was always storming around the neighborhood, muttering under his breath. Or walking down the middle of the road, wearing his pajamas outside in the winter, like he didn't even feel the cold. It's just not natural. Most of the time, he didn't have a clue what he was doing."

"As I understand it, Mr. Penders had dementia," I said.

"As if that's an excuse," Becky sniffed. "Man like that should have been locked away somewhere, not allowed to run around loose in the real world, terrorizing innocent people."

Terrorizing seemed like a strong word. "Who did he terrorize?"

"Everyone!" Becky threw her hands in the air for emphasis. "Whoever he came in contact with. And don't even get me started on that daughter of his."

"What was the matter with her?"

"You ever meet her?"

I shook my head. I'd never met Ralph Penders either.

"Madison, that's her name. I asked her once if she was named after that fish in the movie with Daryl Hannah. She told me it wasn't a fish, it was a mermaid. Like I would care about the difference." She cackled under her breath. "Who would name a kid after a fish anyway?"

Becky didn't appear to want an answer, so I didn't offer one. Which was good. Because I would have told her that Ralph Penders was obviously the kind of person who would do such a thing. And that Madison was a *mermaid*.

"So Ralph was a problem, and you don't like Madison either," I said to recap.

"Now you're just making me sound bad." Becky frowned. "It's not my fault that the two of them were trouble."

"Both of them?"

"Madison was supposed to be watching out for her father because he wasn't fit to be living alone. Huh! Like that ever happened. Maybe she cooked him a meal sometimes, but most days she was nowhere to be found."

"Maybe she has a job," I said.

"Her job should have been taking care of her father," Becky retorted. "One day, Ralph came wandering over here and tripped on a rake Bill left sitting out in the yard. Ralph skinned his knee pretty bad. Madison had to rush back in the middle of the day and take him to Urgent Care. When they got home, she came flying over here like the whole thing was our fault."

Becky's eyes narrowed. "Bill tried to calm her down, but she wasn't having it. Madison threatened to sue us for leaving a dangerous object lying around. Right in our own yard! Can you believe that?"

"It does sound kind of nutty," I admitted.

"So I threatened to sue Ralph right back for trespassing. 'Tit for tat,'" I told her. "'And we'll see you in court.'"

"Did she sue you?" I asked.

"Oh hell, no. That woman doesn't have the brains God gave a pig. She probably consulted some ambulance-chasing lawyer, who told her she didn't have a hope of making the complaint stick."

Becky sat back in her seat, looking pleased. She'd

enjoyed telling her story, and highlighting the part she'd played in it. Her gaze flicked once more toward the television, where a commercial was now playing. A harried-looking housewife was trying to sell soap.

"Wait a minute!" Becky suddenly straightened. "You shouldn't have let me get sidetracked like that. You said you had something to tell me about Harriet. She's in trouble, right?"

"I'm afraid she is. The police spoke with some of Ralph's neighbors. Did they talk to you too?"

She nodded.

"Did they mention how he died?"

"No. I just know he was in the hospital. I figured Ralph died of insanity. Or maybe general orneriness."

"That wasn't it," I told her. "He was poisoned. He died after eating one of Harriet's marshmallow puffs."

"Well, I'll be." Becky grinned. "Way to go, Harriet."

"Except that Harriet wasn't responsible."

Her grin died. Becky liked her own version of events better than mine. "Then who was?"

"I don't know. That's what the police are trying to determine."

"What does that have to do with you?"

There didn't seem to be any point in admitting that I was on Harriet's side, and trying to help her. So instead I said, "Harriet told me that she'd handed out several batches of marshmallow puffs to her neighbors."

"She did," Becky agreed. "We got one too."

"I need to get them back," I said.

"Oh no, you don't. Halloween's coming and I—" Abruptly Becky stopped speaking. "Wait a minute! Are you trying to tell me that my puffs might be poisoned too?"

The end of her question ended on a sharp scream. Before I could answer, she'd already jumped to her feet.

"Probably not," I said. "It's just a—"

Before I could finish, Becky had already run from the room. Her kitchen was right around the corner. I heard the sound of a freezer door opening, then slamming shut.

Seconds later, she was back. Becky was carrying a large plastic tub in her arms. There was frozen condensation on the sides, and the container's top was sealed tight.

"Here. Take it! Get it out of my house!"

She thrust the heavy tub at me. When I didn't raise my hands fast enough, she tossed the container in my direction. I just managed to grab it before it fell.

Becky ran to the door and yanked it open. "Get out! And take that poison with you!"

I was barely on the stoop before she slammed the

door behind me. The pane of glass rattled in its frame. She was lucky it didn't shatter.

Faith was sitting up on the Volvo's backseat. She watched me walk down the sidewalk to the car. I suspected she'd been sitting up for a while, and that she'd seen me get thrown out of Becky Gruber's house.

When I opened the Volvo door and set the plastic container on the floor behind the front seat, the big Poodle bounced up and down in place. I could have sworn she was laughing at me.

"Don't you dare say a word," I told her.

Faith was the soul of discretion. Her tail whipped madly back and forth, but otherwise she kept her thoughts to herself.

Good dog.

Kevin's playdate was at a home in backcountry Greenwich. By coincidence, that was also where Aunt Peg lived. I hadn't spoken to her in twenty-four hours. By now, she would be champing at the bit to find out what was happening.

I thanked Kev's hostess profusely and promised to reciprocate soon. As I buckled him into his booster seat, Kev sat back and demanded, "Where to next?"

Life with a busy mother has taught my son that we are almost always on the run to somewhere else.

"We're going to stop and see Aunt Peg," I said.

"Yippee!" Kevin's shriek was loud enough to make Faith's ears flatten against her head. "Will she have cake?"

Aunt Peg was almost as famous for her addiction to sugar as she was for her line of Cedar Crest Standard Poodles. She always had something sweet on hand to offer guests. Even ones who showed up unexpectedly.

"You don't need to have cake in the middle of the afternoon," I told him.

"That's not what Aunt Peg says."

"Aunt Peg isn't a growing boy."

"Aunt Peg is huge," Kev pointed out. "She ate cake and she grew plenty."

Aunt Peg stood nearly six feet tall and had shoulders that would do a shot-putter proud. She could lift a fifty-pound Standard Poodle with one arm, and she slept fewer hours a night than I did. So clearly I was losing this argument.

"Aunt Peg is an exception," I said.

"To what?"

I sighed. "Everything."

Aunt Peg's home was a restored farmhouse that had once been the nucleus of a working farm. The five acres of land that remained with it gave her plenty of room for the handful of dogs that currently lived with her. A busy dog show judge, she was on the road for much of the year. Now she only had one

Standard Poodle "in hair," a young bitch named Coral, whom Davey was handling in the ring.

"That's odd," I said. I had parked the Volvo in Aunt Peg's driveway, but no Poodle posse had come flying down the steps of the house to greet us. Aunt Peg's canine alarm system kept her apprised of all visitors. She usually had the door open before I'd even turned off the car. "Maybe she's not home."

"Nope," said Kevin. "She's home. She's eating cake."

Maybe. But that wouldn't have kept Aunt Peg from coming to the door. On the console beside me, my phone buzzed. It was a text from Aunt Peg.

Saw you drive in. Be right there.

Where are you? I texted back. She didn't answer. Typical.

Kevin, Faith, and I were standing beside the car a minute later when I heard the sound of spinning gravel. I looked out toward the road and saw Aunt Peg go flying past the end of the driveway on a bicycle.

She was steering with one hand on the handlebars. The other hand was clutching the end of a long leash. The leash was attached to Coral, who was trotting along smartly beside her.

"Wheee!" she cried as she went speeding by.

"Wow!" Davey's eyes widened. "Aunt Peg's riding a bike. Cool."

My stomach dropped. That was so *not cool.*

Roadworking a dog built muscle and fitness for the

show ring. There were different methods, but most people now used treadmills. Roadworking a dog from a bicycle was a young person's game. Aunt Peg was seventy. She could kill herself doing that.

Kevin, Faith, and I ran to the end of the driveway together. Kev was clapping his hands with glee. Faith wanted to go run with Coral. I was just hoping I wouldn't have to scrape Aunt Peg off the macadam when we got there.

The pair traveled another quarter mile down the quiet lane before making a graceful turnaround. Then they came heading back in our direction. It made me nervous to watch Aunt Peg, so I focused on Coral instead. The Poodle bitch had a beautiful way of moving. She was so well balanced that her stride appeared to cover the ground effortlessly.

Coral was wearing the continental clip. The front half of her body was covered by a dense coat of black hair. Her face, hindquarter, legs, and feet were shaved to the skin, except for rosettes on her hips and rounded bracelets on her lower legs.

In the show ring, the long hair on Coral's head would have been banded and sprayed into a high, towering topknot. Now it was wrapped and bound up in ponytails to keep it out of her way. The big Poodle appeared to be enjoying her exercise.

Aunt Peg coasted the last twenty feet between us. When the bike came to a stop, she removed her feet from the pedals and braced the frame on either side. Coral waited impatiently until Aunt Peg had unsnapped her leash. Then she came bounding over to us.

Faith and Coral had met many times before. Now the two Poodles only touched noses briefly before spinning around and dashing away. Kevin went running after them.

"Whew." Aunt Peg expelled a long breath. "That was fun."

"Fun?" I stared at her. "Are you crazy?"

"I sincerely doubt it."

"You could have been killed."

"I sincerely doubt that too." Aunt Peg hopped off the seat. She grasped the bike's handlebars and began to walk up the driveway. "Hardly anybody dies from riding a bike up and down a quiet lane."

"They might if they were attached to a dog. You're not even wearing a helmet."

She gave me a baleful look. "I rode bicycles for decades before people even knew what helmets were. I think I know what I'm doing."

That was the problem with Aunt Peg. She always thought she knew what she was doing.

"What if Coral saw a squirrel and took off? She could have pulled you right over."

"That wasn't going to happen," Aunt Peg said calmly.

"How do you know?"

"Because I train my Poodles to listen to me, like any responsible dog owner should do. Seriously, Melanie, are you sure you want to continue this conversation?"

Actually, I wasn't. For one thing, any minute it was going to turn into a lecture. And for another, now that Aunt Peg had both feet on the ground and I knew she was safe, I was feeling much better.

It was probably wiser to simply put the whole alarming episode behind me. Pretend it had never happened—or at least that I'd never seen it happen.

Aunt Peg wasn't going to take my advice. She never did.

"You're right," I said with a sigh. "Let's just go eat cake."

Chapter
Ten

"Tell me everything," Aunt Peg said.

We were settled at her kitchen table. Her Standard Poodles and Faith were milling around the room. A mocha cake was on the tabletop in front of us.

"Cake first," Kev piped up.

Aunt Peg paused in the act of cutting the cake to dab a smear of icing on his nose. Kev giggled happily. The two of them made a fine pair.

"I was talking to your mother," Aunt Peg told him. "She and I have important things to discuss. Shall I set you up in the other room with a tray and a cartoon?"

"Yes, please." Kevin slid down off his chair. "Can the dogs come too?"

"Only if you promise not to feed them cake." Aunt Peg winked at him as they left the room. "Otherwise there won't be enough for the rest of us."

"You're a bad influence," I told her when she returned. "Cake? Midafternoon television? Reckless bike riding?"

"Oh pish," she replied. "I did all that when I was his age, and I survived."

Of course she had. Aunt Peg would probably survive a zombie apocalypse. And emerge unscathed at the end as the fearless leader.

While she was gone, I'd cut two more slices of cake and placed them on the plates in front of us. "Talk," Aunt Peg commanded as she picked up her fork and dug in.

Quickly I summed up everything that had happened since we'd last spoken. Had it truly been less than a single day? It seemed much longer than that.

"Harriet's in quite a quandary," Aunt Peg said at the end. "Do you think Russell would really fire her?"

"I don't know. He depends on her. We all do. But Mr. Hanover would do anything to protect Howard Academy. If it came down to having to choose between the school's well-being or Harriet's, well . . ." I stopped and sighed. "He might feel forced into doing it, whether he wanted to or not."

We pondered that and ate more cake.

"Tell me more about John Vidal," Aunt Peg said after a minute. "I like the sound of him."

"He applied for a scholarship to Howard Academy and didn't get one." I was talking and eating at the same time. Thank goodness Kev wasn't there to see it. One bad influence a day was plenty.

"Pity, that. He sounds like a bright young man."

"He is. Apparently he knows just about everything there is to know about computers."

"I think you should introduce me," Aunt Peg decided. "I'd imagine he's a useful person to know."

"Maybe you and he can bond over a plate of Harriet's marshmallow puffs," I suggested.

"I'm game if he is." She eyed the cake as if debating helping herself to another piece, then pushed her plate away. "So now what?"

"Back to school tomorrow morning," I told her. "I'll check in with Harriet. I want to see if she has a lawyer yet. I also need to find out what she wants me to do with the puffs I'm gathering up. I expect to retrieve the remaining batches tomorrow afternoon."

Aunt Peg smiled. "It's nice to see you're keeping yourself busy."

The previous morning, Harriet had been waiting in my classroom when I arrived. This morning, I returned the favor. Since she and I were supposed to be working as a team, it made sense for me to keep her up to date on what I was doing.

First I dropped Kev off in the kindergarten classroom with a juice box and an apple. Jill was busy getting things set up for the day. She said she wouldn't mind keeping an eye on him.

Then Faith and I went to the front hall and waited for Harriet to appear. I knew she'd be early. She always was. Harriet was already shedding her woolen coat as she entered the mansion. I stood up and forestalled that.

"Let's walk," I said, offering her a choice of the two coffees I'd picked up at Starbucks.

Harriet grabbed the espresso, leaving me with the mocha latte. She held the front door open for Faith and me. Of one accord, we headed down the hill toward the athletic fields. This time of morning, they were deserted. When Faith grabbed a stick off the ground and ran on ahead of us, I let her go.

"Have you met with your lawyer yet?" I asked.

"Yes. Yesterday afternoon." Harriet removed the plastic top from her cup and took a sip, then nodded her head in approval.

"What's he like?"

"Stern. Serious. Well educated. His name is Reginald Gordon and it suits him. He looks like a man who means business."

"Good. That's what you need." The latte had left a trail of froth across my upper lip. I paused to lick it off. "Will he sit in while Detective Young interrogates you?"

Harriet nodded. She flashed a brief smile. "Except

that he called it an interview, not an interrogation. Mr. Gordon was very clear about that. He was also adamant that I'm not supposed to say anything to anyone about the case."

"Including me?"

She hesitated, then replied, "Technically, yes. But what he doesn't know won't hurt him. After all, I can hardly refuse to answer your questions, can I? Not when we're working together on the case."

Harriet stopped walking, so I did too. Together we stared out over the school's extensive grounds and the town of Greenwich beyond them. From this high vantage point, we could see the traffic on the Post Road.

"Did you find out anything yesterday afternoon?" she asked.

"I talked to your sister. And I met Hugh."

"Bernie's boyfriend." Harriet's lips thinned. "What did you think of him?"

"He seemed nice enough."

"He is that." She shrugged. "Nice, I mean. I just hope Bernie isn't letting herself get too involved."

"How come?"

"My sister is a babe in the woods when it comes to men. I guess she probably told you about Seth?"

I nodded. "She mentioned him."

"They were married for nearly thirty years. They

met very young. It was the only serious relationship Bernie's ever had with a man. After Seth died, there wasn't anyone else. Not for years."

Harriet sighed. "Then I got home from work one day and Hugh was there. Bernie was fluttering around him, acting as giddy as a girl. It all seemed rather sudden to me. She thinks things are serious between them, but I'm not sure Hugh feels the same way. She's happy now, but I'd hate to see her get hurt."

Faith dove beneath a nearby hedge and came up with a lacrosse ball in her mouth. We both watched as she tossed her prize up in the air, then ran after it when it bounced away.

"After I talked to Bernie, I met your neighbor John Vidal," I said.

"He's a good kid."

"That was my impression too." My latte was cooling. I took a long swallow. "He wouldn't give back your marshmallow puffs, though. He said he'd already eaten some and he wanted to finish the rest."

Harriet laughed. "That sounds like John. He sees himself as a contrarian. I'm sure he'll be fine."

"Becky Gruber had the opposite reaction. She just about threw the puffs at me when I told her why I needed them."

"I'm not surprised to hear that. Becky can be a piece of work," Harriet said. "Some days I wonder how Bill puts up with her. The only reason I give her any marshmallow puffs at all is because it helps me stay on her good side. Especially in a small neighborhood like mine, she's not the kind of woman I'd want to have as an enemy."

Faith was still playing with the ball. She brought it to me and I threw it back in the direction of the school. It was time for us to head inside. The Poodle went flying up the incline. Harriet and I followed more sedately.

"I'll have more time this afternoon," I said. "I'm planning to pick up the other batches you handed out. What do you want me to do with them?"

"Just drop them back at my house." Harriet shook her head. I imagined she was thinking of all her hard work going to waste. "I guess I'll have to throw them all in the trash."

We'd reached the wide stone steps. I hopped up and opened the front door. "Two days to go. How's the Halloween party coming along?"

"Cheryl and I have everything under control." Harriet finished her espresso and she crumpled her empty coffee cup in her hand. "Cheryl's great. She's hardly left anything for me to do."

Faith trotted across the gravel driveway. She came up the steps and we entered the mansion together. When I glanced around the wide hall, I realized that the door to the headmaster's office was open. It had been closed when we left. It was almost always closed.

"Ahh, there you are." Mr. Hanover appeared in his doorway. His gaze went straight to Harriet.

She and I shared a look. The headmaster never arrived this early.

"Yes, I'm here." She quickly shrugged out of her coat and hung it in the closet. "Do you need something?"

"I was going to ask you to locate Ms. Travis. But now I see that you've already done so. Truly, you are a marvel of efficiency."

"Thank you, sir."

Harriet looked as baffled as I felt. This probably didn't bode well.

Mr. Hanover beckoned in my direction. "Ms. Travis, a word?"

"Of course." As I scrambled to obey, Harriet moved to intercept Faith. She cupped her hand around the Poodle's muzzle, just as she'd seen me do.

"Faith and I will return the lacrosse ball to the athletic department," Harriet told me. "Then I'll put her in your classroom."

"Thanks," I whispered as I scooted through the doorway.

I wondered what my infraction was this time. Using espresso to lure his assistant away from her post before the first bell? Not keeping a close enough eye on Eddie Mackelroy? Running around the mansion's attic without permission? It seemed a shame there were so many possibilities to choose from.

Mr. Hanover was already seated behind his desk. "Close the door behind you, please."

Sure. That made me feel better.

"Have a seat."

A club chair had been positioned to face the headmaster's desk. I sat.

I folded my hands demurely in my lap. I waited while Mr. Hanover perused some papers on his blotter. I admired the man's maroon-and-navy repp tie. Then I stared at the coffered ceiling for a few seconds.

If Mr. Hanover meant to keep me waiting until I began to sweat, he'd already achieved his aim. Another minute of this and I'd be willing to confess to almost anything.

Then the headmaster looked up. Our eyes met. I willed myself not to squirm in my seat. I was an adult. I could do this.

"Am I correct in understanding that you and Detective Young have developed a cordial relationship?" he asked.

Okay, I hadn't expected that. Nor was I sure how to answer the question. *Cordial* implied that the detective and I were friends, which we most certainly were not. We had, however, managed to work together on an occasion or two in the past.

"Umm . . . yes?" I replied.

Mr. Hanover steepled his hands beneath his chin. "Good."

Good?

"I'd like you to do something for me."

"Of course."

The headmaster smiled. "Don't you want to hear my request first?"

Maybe the man didn't understand the parameters of our power dynamic. To me, they seemed simple. He asked. I acquiesced.

"If you need me to do something, I'm sure there's a good reason for it," I said primly.

"Indeed. I believe you are acquainted with the full extent of Harriet's present problem?"

"I am, but—"

Mr. Hanover held up a hand. Immediately I stopped speaking. Pavlov would have been proud.

"Whatever the capacity in which you may have become involved in that situation, it's better if I don't know the details," he said.

I got it. He wanted plausible deniability. I nodded. Then I spoke up anyway.

"I only wanted to say that any poking around I might or might not be doing is taking place on my own time. And well away from school grounds."

That hadn't always been the case in the past. This

time, I wanted to make sure he and I understood each other.

"As it should be," the headmaster concurred. "I would like to see this business with Harriet wrapped up as soon as possible. I got the impression from Detective Young that the police view Harriet as a very viable suspect. Two days have passed since that time. The authorities are obviously under no obligation to keep us apprised about their investigation. Nevertheless, I would like to know if any further progress has been made."

Mr. Hanover paused. It felt like he was waiting for me to speak. Unfortunately I had no idea what he wanted me to say.

"Perhaps you could find out?" he prompted.

I swallowed. "You want me to ask Detective Young about his investigation?"

"Indeed."

"Wouldn't that . . ." I cleared my throat and started again. "Wouldn't that be something for Harriet's lawyer to do?"

"I don't believe it's in our best interests to make an official inquiry. I thought perhaps you could approach him as a friend."

That might have been possible—if the detective and I had actually been friends. That inconvenient fact had no bearing on my answer, however. Because, you know, power dynamic.

"I could try," I said.

"Excellent. Do so."

Mr. Hanover rose from his seat and walked around the desk. By the time he reached me, I was standing too. He escorted me to the office door and opened it.

"I'm glad we're on the same page, Ms. Travis. I look forward to hearing from you."

Harriet looked at me and raised a brow. As soon as Mr. Hanover's back was turned, I gave her a small shrug.

Same page? Mr. Hanover and I were barely in the same library.

Now I had another assignment to pencil into my busy schedule.

Chapter
Eleven

That morning, I'd planned ahead and arranged for Sam to pick up Kevin when his kindergarten class was dismissed at one o'clock. Faith would go home with them too. That left me free to go straight back to Glenville. This time, I'd have the whole afternoon to spend talking to Harriet's other neighbors.

The next address on my list belonged to Kent and Judy Upchurch. The couple lived several doors down from John Vidal. I parked on the street in front of Harriet's house.

When I got out of the Volvo, I saw that someone was outside in front of the Upchurches' home. A man dressed in worn jeans and a checked flannel jacket was brushing debris off the front walk. I strolled over to say hello.

A low picket fence bordered the small yard. Three giant rubber spiders with ghoulish faces were arranged across the top of the gate. Just looking at the trio made me shudder.

I stopped well clear of the arachnids and said, "Excuse me, I'm looking for Kent Upchurch?"

The man stopped working. He set his broom upright and folded his hands on top of the handle. Up close, he was older than I'd thought. His skin had been weathered by the years and tufts of gray hair stuck out from beneath his Yankees ball cap.

"Could be you've found him. Who're you?"

"Melanie Travis. I'm a friend of the Bloom sisters."

"You probably mean Harriet." He nodded. "I was expecting someone to show up and ask more questions. We heard all about what happened from Becky. She's probably told half of Glenville by now. I guess you want those marshmallow puffs back? Damn shame about that."

I wasn't sure whether he was referring to the loss of the puffs or Harriet's problems, but it was easy enough to agree to both.

"It is a shame. And, yes, I do want the puffs back. Harriet thinks that's safer."

Kent snorted. "Safety and liability. Seems like that's all anyone worries about these days. Judy and I have been handing out those treats on Halloween for nearly twenty years. They're kind of famous around here.

Trick-or-treaters come down this street on purpose just to get them."

"They're famous at Harriet's place of work too," I told him.

"Howard Academy, right?"

"Yes."

"And you work there too?"

I almost laughed. Gossip traveled fast around here.

"I do," I confirmed.

"Good for you. Education is important. Best thing parents can do to invest in their children's future."

"Do you have children?"

"Two. But they're grown up and gone now. One's in Boston and the other is based in London. Got a call just the other day asking if our supply of marshmallow treats had arrived yet." Kent smiled thinking about it. Then abruptly his smile faded. "Sure seems odd to me. I can't imagine why Harriet wanted to kill Ralph. The old guy wasn't *that* much trouble."

I stared at him, surprised. "What makes you think she did?"

"That's what Becky told me. Said she'd heard the news from a good source."

I frowned. "Did she say who that was?"

"Nope. Just that she did it by feeding him a poisoned puff."

"She didn't," I told him firmly. "Harriet didn't kill Ralph that way or any other way. She's innocent."

He squinted at me across the yard. "You think so?"

"I do."

"And yet here you are, wanting to grab back our treats anyway. That doesn't sound to me like you believe what you're saying."

I gritted my teeth, managing to make it look like a smile. "Maybe you could go inside and get your marshmallow puffs for me? I'll wait right here until you come back."

"Won't do you much good," Kent informed me. "We don't have 'em anymore. The whole batch is gone."

"Gone where?"

"After Becky called around with the news yesterday, Judy packed up our bin and took it to the dump. She wouldn't let me try a single puff. Even when I asked nicely." He slipped me a wink. "I told her I figured our batch must be safe enough. After all, it wasn't as though we'd done anything lately to tick off those Bloom sisters."

He laughed under his breath, like that was a pretty good joke. Then he picked up his broom and resumed sweeping.

I thought about what Kent Upchurch had just said. "Wait a minute. Had Ralph Penders done something that Harriet or Bernadette was upset about?"

I knew he must have heard the question, but Kent didn't respond. When I asked a second time, he angled his body away so that his back was facing me. He continued sweeping without missing a beat. That dismissal was clear enough.

"Hellooo!"

A young woman waved to me from the other side of the road. Dressed in a red tracksuit and sneakers, she was standing on the sidewalk behind a stroller whose occupant was bundled up from head to toe. I crossed the street to see what she wanted.

"Hey, are you Melanie?" The woman smiled. Her fingers were resting on the stroller's handlebar; her nails were bitten down to the quick. "I'm Trixie Dent. I live next door to the Blooms."

"Nice to meet you. I stopped by your house yesterday afternoon, but no one was home."

"Yeah, my husband was at work and I was probably out running around with this guy."

She reached around the stroller's canopy and flipped back a blue blanket. A baby who looked to be about six months old gave me a gummy grin.

"That's Wyatt. If we sit in the house, he won't sleep. As soon as I get him moving, he's out like a light."

"Hi, Wyatt."

The baby was chewing happily on a set of rubber keys. I gave him a wave, which he ignored. Trixie quickly tucked the blanket in again.

"I heard you're talking to everyone," she said. "Do

you want to walk with me? It's less than a mile around the block. If we keep moving, it should take about ten minutes."

"Sure, let's go." I fell into step beside her. "I guess you heard about me from Becky Gruber?"

"No, actually from Bernadette. Our backyards share a fence. We were both outside last evening and we got to talking. She told me about the police being on Harriet's case because of her marshmallow puffs. Wyatt keeps me pretty busy, so that was the first I'd heard about Ralph dying from anything other than natural causes. It's crazy that the police suspect Harriet."

"I agree. It would help to clear her if the police had someone else to focus on. Do you know why anyone might have wanted to harm Ralph?"

"That's a tough one." Trixie steered the stroller carefully around a break in the sidewalk. "I didn't know him very well. Mostly because we weren't living here before . . . you know."

"Before he got dementia?"

She nodded. "Apparently he was an interesting guy when he was younger. A chemist working in pharmaceutical research. But he'd been retired for a while. Mostly he just hung around his house."

"Or the neighborhood?" I asked.

"That too. It was better when he was inside his home, because Ralph was apt to lose his way when he came out here." Her hand gesture encompassed the block. "Also, he seemed to have forgotten how to look out for traffic. I was always afraid that someday he'd really get hurt."

And then he had, I thought.

"It sounds as though Ralph shouldn't have been living on his own," I said. "Did he have a home care nurse?"

"No, nothing like that." Trixie frowned. "I don't think there was enough money for that kind of supervision. Ralph had a daughter, Madison. She was supposed to stop in and check on him every day."

"Supposed to?"

"I hate to complain, but truthfully? I don't think she was nearly as diligent as she should have been. I mean, we've been living here more than a year and Ralph was right next door, so I couldn't help but pay attention. It seemed like most weeks, Madison stopped by once or twice at best."

"That doesn't sound like much oversight for a man in his condition."

"It wasn't nearly enough," she agreed. "Although I'm sure the situation was hard on her too. Even when Madison was around, things weren't always rosy. Last summer, when our windows were open, there were times when I'd hear him yelling at her. I mean, really berating her, you know?"

I nodded.

"I'm not sure she'd even done anything wrong. It just sounded like he was frustrated. Or bitter about his situation. It was almost as if he blamed her for his condition."

For the second time, we reached the end of a block, and turned right. We were halfway back to where we'd started.

"I was just talking to your neighbor across the road," I said.

"Kent?" Trixie laughed. "Yeah, he's a character."

"He implied that something had happened between Ralph and the Bloom sisters. Something that might have made Harriet angry. Do you know anything about that?"

She thought briefly, then shook her head. "Nope. I don't have any idea. Aside from his daughter, Ralph didn't fight with anyone else. Most of the time, I don't think he really remembered who the rest of us were."

We kept strolling. I let her think some more.

"Madison, though," Trixie said after a few minutes. "She and Harriet didn't get along."

If I had been a Poodle, I'd have pricked my ears. "How come?"

"Harriet thought that Madison should be doing more for her father. I mean, we *all* thought that. But Harriet was the only one who stood up and told her so."

"Did it make a difference?"

"No, unfortunately. Not one that I saw anyway. Madison told Harriet to mind her own business. She was pissed. But Harriet was too. After that, it seemed to me like the two of them had a standoff going on. Neither one was ever going to admit that she was wrong."

We made another turn. Now we were back on the road where we'd started originally. I pulled out my list and looked for the next address. Trixie leaned over and had a look, too. Her finger stabbed at one couple's names.

"You can cross off the Jennings," she said. "They're away on a two-week cruise through Scandinavia. They won't be back until after Halloween."

That meant there was just one name remaining: Cynthia Lewis. I'd hoped that talking to Harriet's neighbors would help me learn more about Ralph—and point me toward figuring out who'd wanted to kill him. But right now, things didn't seem any clearer to me than they had in the beginning.

"You'll like Cynthia," Trixie told me. "Although I should warn you, she's a fanatic when it comes to Harriet's marshmallow puffs. If you want to get hers back, you might have to wrestle them away from her. Every year, Cynthia says she's going to hand those things out to trick-or-treaters. And every year, they're gone by the time the holiday arrives because she's already eaten them all herself."

"I hope she hasn't eaten this batch," I said. "Speaking of which, I need yours back too."

"Don't worry about that. I already took care of them. I handed them over the fence to Bernadette last night. I'm not as much of a fanatic as Cynthia, but you better believe I was sorry to see them go."

Trixie pointed out Cynthia Lewis's house. Then she and Wyatt continued on their walk. I stood on a small front porch beside a festive display of pumpkins, squash, and colored corn, and rang the doorbell. When Cynthia answered, she didn't look surprised to see a strange woman standing outside her door. By now, the whole neighborhood must have known what I was up to.

Cynthia invited me in and we conducted our short conversation standing in her front hall. As Trixie had predicted, I did like her. Cynthia was warm and funny, and used lots of big gestures when she spoke. Having been an off-Broadway actress in her younger years, Cynthia now did voice-over work for commercials and cartoons.

"It pays the bills beautifully," she said with a laugh. "But imagine having to figure out what a talking toilet brush should sound like. Or a hungry cat. I bet you've seen the singing popcorn ball? That's me too."

Unfortunately for my purposes, Cynthia hadn't known Ralph well. She didn't have any ideas to share regarding possible motives for his death. I waited while she retrieved a parcel of marshmallow puffs from her freezer.

"You're sure you want these back?" she asked regretfully, before handing them over.

"Now that you know the risk you're taking, it's really up to you." I noted that the seal on the package was broken. "Especially if you've already sampled one or two."

"Yeah, one or two." She grinned. "Or maybe eight. And I feel as healthy as a horse."

I started to hand the parcel back, but Cynthia shook her head. "I suppose it's better to be on the safe side. Especially after what happened to Ralph. That poor man didn't deserve to die. I intended to go to his funeral, you know. Even if it meant taking a day off from work. I was afraid the turnout wouldn't be very big, and I wanted to offer my support."

Abruptly I realized that no one else had said a thing about a ceremony for Ralph. "When is it?" I asked.

"That's just it. There isn't going to be one."

"What about a memorial service?"

"Neither one," she confirmed unhappily. "I asked around, but no one seemed to know anything about it. So I called that daughter of his."

"Madison," I said.

"Yes, Madison. We'd all been given her cell number in case of emergency." Cynthia rolled her eyes.

"And because we never knew which one of us might find ourselves tripping over Ralph next."

I didn't want to smile, because this was serious business. But Cynthia had a wonderful way with words.

"She told me there was no point in holding a service for Ralph. That no one would come because everyone he knew was either dead or they'd forgotten him."

"That's cold," I said.

Cynthia crossed her arms over her chest and shivered. Once an actress, always an actress. "Cold doesn't even scratch the surface. That chick's attitude was positively frigid."

Chapter
Twelve

Finally it looked as though I might have a suspect. Or at least the possibility of one. I now knew of someone who'd felt real animosity toward Ralph Penders. That had to count for something—even if that person was his own daughter.

I hadn't met Madison yet, but based on what I'd heard, I already didn't like her. I found myself picturing a nasty-looking woman with a hooked nose and a pointy black hat. Probably because I had Halloween on the brain.

Back at my car, I picked up Becky's marshmallow puffs. Juggling that batch, along with Cynthia's, I didn't have a free hand to knock on the Bloom sisters' door. So I gave it a little kick instead. That was enough to bring Bernadette running.

"Let me help you with those." She grabbed the top parcel out of my hands. "Harry told me you'd be stopping by to drop off more puffs. Is this the last of them?"

"Just about." I leaned against the door to close it behind us. "John Vidal decided to keep his. And apparently the Jennings are away on a cruise. But all the others have been accounted for."

"Good." She led the way to the kitchen. "Harry will be happy about that."

"Speaking of Harriet . . ."

As we entered the room, my voice died away. I'd thought that Bernadette and I were alone. But Hugh was standing in the doorway that led to the dining room.

"What about Harriet?" he asked.

I glanced at Bernadette. She didn't seem to mind that he'd inserted himself into our conversation.

"Hello, Hugh." I wondered why he was always hanging around in the middle of the day. Didn't he have a job?

"You're Melanie, right?"

Hugh stepped forward to take the bundle of marshmallow puffs out of Bernadette's arms. Then he set them down on the counter. Honestly, it had saved her from walking about two feet. But Bernadette looked inordinately pleased by the gesture.

"Yes, Melanie," I told him. We'd just met the day before. I should hope he'd remember my name.

I walked around Hugh and set the package I'd retrieved from the Volvo on top of the other one. Then I turned back to Bernadette. "Do you have a few minutes to talk?"

"Anything to help Harry," she said. "Let's go in the living room and get comfortable."

Together we headed for the arched doorway between the rooms. Bernadette looked to see if Hugh was coming. I hoped he wasn't, but if he wanted to join us, there wasn't much I could do about it.

When I glanced back, I saw that Hugh was opening the top container of marshmallow puffs. Having come from Becky the previous day, the treats had defrosted overnight in my car. He pried up the lid and pulled one out.

"Are you sure you want to do that?" I asked as he lifted it toward his mouth.

He paused to look at me. "Why not? They'll only go to waste."

"The reason Harriet wanted them back was because she was concerned that Ralph's batch wasn't the only one that was contaminated."

"Oh . . . that."

Yes, that, I thought.

"I'm not worried." Hugh popped the puff in his mouth, chewing it with visible enjoyment. He swallowed, then said, "See? Nothing to fear." He winked at Bernadette. "But if I suddenly start frothing at the mouth, call nine-one-one for me, okay?"

"Oh Hugh." She tittered. "You're such a tease."

We got settled in the living room. Bernadette and Hugh sat side by side on a dove-gray sofa. I took a seat opposite them on a matching chair. Hugh's hand slid along the cushion between him and Bernadette until his fingertips were able to graze the outer edge of her thigh.

I frowned and lifted my gaze away. *Seriously?* At their ages, couldn't they save this stuff for when they were alone?

"What did you want to talk about, Melanie?" Bernadette asked. Her voice sounded unnaturally high. I wanted to slap Hugh's hand away so she could concentrate on our conversation.

"Ralph's daughter, Madison," I said. "Did you know her?"

"Of course. Ralph lived in that house for years. I think he and his wife moved in when she was in high school."

"How old was Ralph when he died?" I asked.

"I'm not sure. Maybe in his seventies? Physically, Ralph's health was fine. It was his brain that was . . ." Bernadette lifted a hand and circled it beside her head in a very un-PC gesture. "Madison was their only child. She just turned forty. She had a cake delivered to Ralph's place a few months ago so she and her dad could celebrate together."

Bernadette turned and looked at Hugh. "You remember that, don't you, honey?"

"Hmmm . . ." He smiled at her and shifted his hand. "What?"

"Madison's birthday party?"

"No, I wasn't here."

"You weren't?" She looked surprised.

"Nope. I must have been out of town. I've never met Madison Penders. Nor her father, for that matter."

I attempted to draw Bernadette's attention back to me. "I asked because Kent Upchurch implied there might have been a problem between Ralph and Harriet. Then Trixie Dent wondered if he could have meant Harriet and Madison. Were you aware of any issues between them that I should know about?"

"Well . . ." Bernadette chewed on her lip. "I guess maybe you heard that Harry told Madison she needed to straighten up and fly right?"

"Something like that," I agreed.

"It was no big deal. Harry just said some things she felt needed to be said. Tempers flared up for a minute or two, then everything went right back to normal."

A minute or two? Trixie had implied the disagreement had lasted a lot longer than that.

"Don't forget about the thing with Howard Academy," Hugh said.

Bernadette and I both turned to look at him.

"What thing?" I asked.

"You know." He directed his answer to Bernadette. She still looked puzzled.

"Hugh?"

His gaze came back to me. "That's right, I forgot. You work at Howard Academy, too."

"I do." I didn't recall telling him that yesterday. Maybe Bernadette had mentioned it after I left. "Is that a problem?"

"Not for me." His smile was all charm. "But you know how people can be. Howard Academy styles itself as a school for the children of the rich and famous. The one-percenters. So those who don't have the connections or the money to send their kids there get a skewed idea about the place. They think everyone must be really snooty."

"That's not true," I said.

Hugh shrugged. Like the attitude wasn't *his* fault. He was just the messenger. "Human nature."

I growled under my breath.

"You can see how it would happen," he said. "The school's always popping up in the press, usually in connection with some senator or Hollywood director. People get ideas."

"Howard Academy offers kids a great education," I told him. "That's why high-achieving parents send their kids there."

"So they can mix with their own kind."

"No, so they can get their kids' academic careers off to a great start."

"You see?" Hugh grinned. "You're doing it yourself."

"Doing what?"

"Academic career," he repeated. "How pretentious is that? Most kids just go to school. They don't make a *career* of it."

"Baby, that's enough." Bernadette was smiling, but she didn't look happy.

"You know I have a point," he said.

"What I know is that you've had this argument with Harry, too," she retorted. "And that there's no winning it for either of you. Now apologize to Melanie and play nice."

"I'm sorry." Hugh didn't sound sorry in the slightest. "I didn't mean to lecture you on the plight of the working class."

He was a fine one to talk. From his Gucci loafers to his Ralph Lauren pullover, there was nothing working class about Hugh's appearance. I shoved that thought aside. He'd mentioned something earlier, and I needed to get back to it.

"You said something a minute ago," I told him. "About Howard Academy and Ralph, or maybe it was Madison?"

"Right." Hugh nodded. "Bernie, you tell her."

"Tell Melanie what?" she asked.

"About Madison wanting to apply for a job, and Harriet refusing to pull strings for her. Come on, babe, you told me this story."

"I did? I don't remember that." Bernadette turned back to me. "Anyway, what Hugh said is about the gist of it. Just like the other thing, it wasn't important. They had a conversation about it, and then it was over and done with."

Maybe. But I'd be sure to ask Harriet about both issues later.

I rose to my feet. "I'd like to talk with Madison Penders myself," I said to Bernadette. "Could you give me her phone number?"

She jumped up. "I have it written down in the kitchen. I'll go get it for you."

"I really am sorry," Hugh said when she'd left the room. "I didn't mean to go off on you like that. Please accept my apology, or I'll never hear the end of it from Bernie."

"Don't worry about it. I wasn't offended by what you said. I just didn't agree. Bernadette seems like a really nice person."

"She is," Hugh said. "I'm lucky to have found her."

"I certainly wouldn't want to cause any problems between you."

"Problems?" Bernadette caught the tail end of what I was saying. "What's the matter now?"

"Nothing." Hugh smiled expansively. "Melanie and I were just kissing and making up."

Bernadette gave me a coy look. "I certainly hope you weren't kissing my honey bunny."

"No, of course not." That had been an awkward choice of words on Hugh's part. "There was definitely no kissing."

She handed me a piece of paper with Madison's phone number on it, and walked me to the door. "I knew that," she whispered. "I was just teasing you. Hugh doesn't have eyes for anyone else but me."

As I walked back to the Volvo, I hoped Bernadette was right. I agreed with Harriet. I would hate to see her get hurt.

I arrived home just as Davey's school bus was stopping at the end of the driveway. As I waited for the bus to drive on, Davey saw me, doubled back, and opened the car door. He tossed his backpack on the floor, then hopped in the passenger seat.

I gave my son a baleful look. "Is the driveway too long a walk for you?"

"Why should I walk when I can ride?" he asked. "Besides, my backpack's heavy."

"You must have lots of homework to do tonight."

Davey shrugged. And quickly changed the subject. "Where were you this afternoon? Out buying stuff for the munchkin's Halloween costume?"

Yikes. It was a good thing he'd reminded me. Time was passing and I still hadn't done a thing.

"What does Kevin want to be now?" I asked. The two boys discussed Kev's options endlessly.

"This morning, it was Steve Jobs. You know, the founder of Apple?"

"I know who Steve Jobs is." I stared at Davey across the seat. "But how does Kevin know?"

"I told him. I figured it might make your life a little easier."

"Thank you." The reply was automatic. Every mother appreciates that thought. But then I had to ask, "How?"

"Think about it, Mom." Davey grinned. "How hard can it be to come up with a black turtleneck?"

The Poodles and Bud met us in the hallway when we entered the house from the garage. All six dogs were happy to see us, so general pandemonium ensued. Each Poodle wanted to be properly greeted and told that he or she was the best dog in the world. Bud didn't care about that. He was just hoping I'd be handing out dog biscuits.

Okay, so I'm a soft touch. I took the pack to the kitchen so I could give out biscuits. Sam and Kevin were sitting at the kitchen table, working on a jigsaw puzzle.

Sam looked up as we walked in. "The happy wanderer has returned," he said.

"The what?" I stared at him.

That brief moment of inattention was all Bud needed to snatch a biscuit, which had been intended for Eve, out of my hand. The little dog grabbed it and ran. In seconds, he'd be under the couch.

"Sorry, girl." I handed her another one. "Never mind," I said to Sam. It was probably better if I didn't know.

"Dad's making hamburgers for dinner," Kev announced. "We got out the grill and everything."

Sam loved his grill beyond all reason. I'd long since given up trying to understand their connection. It had to be a man thing.

"Are you helping?" I asked Kevin.

He nodded eagerly. "I'm in charge of the buns."

"Okay by you?" Sam asked.

That answer was easy. "As long as you're cooking, you're the boss," I said.

Chapter
Thirteen

After dinner, Sam and the boys parked themselves in front of the TV with a video game. I had calls to make. I grabbed my phone, and Faith and I went upstairs.

She jumped on the bed, made a nest in the pillows, and lay down. I closed the bedroom door behind us. When I joined her on the bed, Faith's tail thumped up and down on the duvet.

She nudged a pillow my way. Using it meant I had to move closer to her. Now Faith and I were side by side. That pleased both of us.

First I called Madison Penders's number. She didn't pick up. She probably thought I was another robo-call. I left her a lengthy message explaining who I was and asked her to call me back.

The second person I tried was Harriet. She answered right away.

"Are you busy?" I asked.

"I'm pacing back and forth in my living room, waiting to see if Detective Young and his minions are going to come and arrest me."

That sounded dire. "Do you think they might?"

"It could happen."

"What does Reginald have to say about that?"

"That he will do everything in his power to make sure it doesn't happen. Blah, blah, legalese, big words. You know."

"Oh." That didn't sound reassuring. "Is this a result of your interview-slash-interrogation? I assume Reggie went to the police station with you?"

"It is, and he did. Mostly, we just sat there and declined to say a word. I don't see how that's a productive exercise for either side, but apparently it's the way the game is played."

"Except it's not a game, it's your life," I said.

"Yes." She sighed. "I know."

I snuggled into the bed. Then I felt guilty for making myself even more comfortable when Harriet's life was falling apart. So I pinched myself on the arm. *Ouch,* that hurt.

Faith stared at me like I was crazy. She was probably right.

"I wanted to ask you about your relationship with Ralph, and his daughter, Madison," I said.

"We were neighbors," Harriet replied. "Cordial, but not particularly close. We waved when we saw each other on the street and we exchanged Christmas cards every year."

"You were close enough to bake Ralph a batch of marshmallow puffs," I mentioned.

"Now you sound like the police," she muttered.

"That's a good thing. Because it means I'm on the same track they are. Hopefully, we'll both reach the same conclusion—that you're innocent."

"I give marshmallow puffs to lots of people," Harriet said. "This time of year, I hand out those things willy-nilly. Everyone from the mailman to Trixie's lawn service guy gets some."

"Trixie has a lawn service guy?" Her yard was a fraction the size of ours. I wished we had a lawn service guy. "Sorry, segue," I said out loud. "Continue."

"This year, aside from the batches I baked early, I haven't given any others away. For obvious reasons."

"What about Madison?" I asked.

"What about her?"

"I heard the two of you had problems with each other."

"It was nothing," Harriet said quickly.

Which, of course, only made me want to hear more.

"You're sure about that?"

"Yes."

Her tone was sharp. The reply, clipped and to the

point. It was the kind of answer Reginald Gordon might have allowed her to give if he'd been presiding over our conversation. Thank goodness he wasn't, because I wanted more.

"Harriet, you're not talking to the police now. This is me, your partner. We're supposed to be working together, remember?"

She didn't say anything.

I kept talking. "You sent me to speak with your neighbors. You wanted me to learn things. And I did. That was the whole point, right?"

"I guess," she replied. "But it's still an awful feeling. Imagine if it was your life that was being dissected like this."

"I'd hate it just as much as you do," I agreed. "But right now, we're not worrying about that. We can't *afford* to worry about it. We have bigger problems— like making sure you don't lose your job and keeping you out of jail. Now talk to me."

For a minute, there was only silence. Faith and I played "catch the fingers" on the duvet as I waited Harriet out.

"There was an incident with my mailbox," she said finally.

That wasn't what I'd expected to hear. "What happened?"

"One evening not too long ago, I came home to

find Ralph standing in a big hole in my garden. He told me he was digging an escape tunnel. He was covered in mud, and my front yard was a mess."

I wondered where Bernadette had been while that was going on. Now that Harriet was finally talking, however, I didn't want to interrupt.

"So I took Ralph home. I figured that he was on his own and that I'd probably have to get him settled in for the night. But to my surprise, Madison was at his house. She'd dropped by, and when her father wasn't there, she hadn't bothered to go looking for him."

"I can see why that would make you angry," I said.

"I'm not proud of losing my temper," Harriet admitted. "But I gave her a piece of my mind. I told Madison she needed to step up and start taking care of Ralph because he clearly wasn't capable of caring for himself."

"What did she say to that?"

"Nothing. It was very odd. Madison just stood there and listened to me. When I was finished, she showed me to the door and locked it behind me."

Despite what Bernadette had told me, I knew that wasn't the end of it. I was still waiting to hear the part about the mailbox.

"The next morning when I walked outside to my car, I saw that my hand-painted bluebird mailbox had been smashed to pieces," Harriet said. "It looked as though someone had taken a baseball bat to it."

Well, crap.

"It's almost Halloween," I felt obliged to mention. "In my neighborhood, teenagers have been out playing pranks after dark."

"That's what Bernie said. She pointed out it wasn't the first time we'd had property damage this time of year. But mine was the only mailbox on the whole block that had been touched."

"Did you report the vandalism to the police?"

"There was no point," Harriet said. "I didn't have any proof who had done it."

"But you had your suspicions."

"Not suspicions," she corrected me. "I *knew* who it was. And I was as mad as a wet cat."

We both paused to let that thought sink in.

"I would hardly have killed Madison's father because I was angry over a broken mailbox," Harriet said after a minute.

"It doesn't matter. The police could still use it against you."

"I hadn't thought about that." She sighed. "I suppose I'll have to tell Reginald. When he took me on as a client, he made it quite clear that he hates surprises."

Faith was growing bored. Apparently listening to my conversations with Aunt Peg was more exciting. She leaned over, rested her head on my shoulder, and closed her eyes. Her ear hair tickled my cheek.

"There's something else," I said.

"Now what?" Harriet didn't sound happy.

"Did Madison ask you to help her get a job at Howard Academy?"

"Not exactly. It was more like she kept hinting about what a good fit she would be at HA. Doing what, I have no idea—she didn't specify and I didn't ask. She said that after all the years I've worked there, surely I must have some influence I could use."

"You turned her down," I said. It wasn't a question.

"I tried. She didn't want to hear it. So I started pretending I was deaf whenever the topic came up. Who told you about that?"

"Earlier, when I was talking to your sister, Hugh brought it up."

"*Hugh* did?" Harriet wasn't pleased.

"Yes."

"He was there too?"

"Yes," I confirmed, though it hardly seemed necessary. I couldn't have been talking to him if he wasn't. But Harriet's emphasis on that fact made her annoyance doubly clear.

"There's no reason why Hugh needs to be poking around in my private business," she said flatly. "He has some nerve."

"What does Hugh do for a living?" I asked.

"I don't know exactly. He was vague about the details when I asked. Bernie thinks he's some kind of real estate hotshot. But then, she believes everything he says. Whatever his job is, it seems to leave him plenty of free time to hang around my house."

"Hugh doesn't think much of Howard Academy," I said. "He called it a school for the children of the rich and famous."

"Yes, he does that." Harriet snorted. "Just between us—he's not entirely wrong. But still, the description stings, as I'm sure it's meant to. Denigrating the school is his way of getting back at me."

"For what?" I asked.

"When I first met him, Hugh was fascinated by my connection to HA. He wanted me to tell him all about the wealthy and influential families whose children are enrolled there. He even seemed to think I might be persuaded to arrange an introduction or two. Of course I wasn't having any of that nonsense. I clammed up and refused to play his game."

"He's an idiot," I said.

"I know that. But unfortunately, Bernie doesn't."

It was time to wrap things up.

"So you'll talk to Reginald tomorrow about the things we've discussed?" I asked.

"I guess I'll have to. Frankly, it seems ridiculous. The issues I had with Madison were nothing more than petty squabbles. If Ralph hadn't died, and my life wasn't being examined so minutely, no one would even remember they happened."

I wasn't so sure about that. Trixie remembered. So had Kent and Hugh. If Ralph hadn't died, maybe they wouldn't have spoken about what they knew. But they'd have remembered.

The following morning, I was scheduled to see a new student during third period. There was a quick knock on the door; then it opened right away. Cheryl Feeney came in. She was holding the hand of a small boy. I knew he was a first grader. Even so, he looked very young in his school uniform of navy blue pants, white button-down shirt, and striped tie.

Cheryl smiled at me as they crossed the room. The boy didn't look up. I wondered if he was shy, or just uncomfortable.

"This is Luke Chism," Cheryl said in a cheery voice. "You and he are going to be doing some reading together." She nudged the boy forward. "Luke, isn't there something you'd like to say to Ms. Travis?"

"Nice to meet you, Ms. Travis." He hesitated, then held out his hand for me to shake. He still hadn't looked up.

"It's nice to meet you too, Luke. I'm sure we're going to have fun together."

"I guess so." He sounded like he didn't believe me.

Faith was lying on her bed, watching our interaction with interest. Usually, she waited for me to summon her before coming over to introduce herself. Now, however, she must have realized her presence was needed. The Poodle stood up, stepped daintily off the cedar-stuffed bed, and treated herself to a long, leisurely stretch.

Luke caught the movement out of the corner of his eye. He turned to look and his gaze widened. Faith's tail was already wagging. When she straightened back up again, her head was as high as Luke's shoulder.

"She's beautiful," he said in awe. "What's her name?"

"Faith. She's a Standard Poodle."

"Yes, I know."

He knew? That was different. Nobody ever knew. Cheryl and I shared a look.

"Is it all right if I pet her?" Luke asked eagerly.

"Of course," I said. "She'd like that. Faith is very friendly."

I expected Luke to wait for Faith to approach him. Instead, with a sudden burst of enthusiasm, the boy went scampering over to where the Poodle was standing. Luke held out his hand and waited for Faith to sniff it.

"What a nice dog you are," he crooned. "Do you want to be my friend?"

Faith lowered the front half of her body to the

floor and woofed softly. As her tail whipped from side to side, her whole hindquarter wiggled. That was a definite yes.

When the Poodle popped back up, her head was between Luke's outstretched arms. She licked his chin. Luke buried his face in her thick hair and gave her a hug.

Cheryl stared in astonishment as child and Poodle bonded with one another. I suspected she was reconsidering her initial impression of Faith.

"Now I get it," she said after a minute.

I just smiled. This wasn't the first time I'd watched Faith work her magic. The Poodle had a real gift, and I was grateful every day for her presence in my classroom.

"You don't have to worry about Luke," I said. "He'll be fine here."

"I can see that." Cheryl lowered her voice before continuing. "It's not that he isn't smart, but he's already falling behind in reading. He told me sometimes the letters jump around on the page. He's going to need testing. You'll know what to do."

I did. And I'd be sure to take care of it.

"Is everything all set for the Halloween party tonight?" I asked. "I hope you haven't seen any more ghosts."

"Not a single one. Thank goodness it was you and

not Harriet that I dragged up to the attic to have a look. I'd have hated to appear that dumb in front of her."

"So the two of you are getting along well?"

"Sure, Harriet's great." Cheryl leaned in and confided, "I know she couldn't have done those things the police suspect her of doing."

I looked at her in surprise. "Did Harriet tell you about that?"

"Of course not. Harriet's very discreet. And I wouldn't dream of bringing up the topic in her presence. But the news is all over the school. Everybody's whispering about it."

How did everyone know about Harriet's problems? I wondered when Cheryl had left. The media hadn't named a suspect in their stories. I wasn't talking. Harriet wasn't talking. I knew for sure that Mr. Hanover wasn't talking. So how had the news gotten out?

Chapter
Fourteen

When Luke's tutoring session ended, Faith and I escorted him back to his first-grade classroom. The little boy walked the entire way with his small hand resting on Faith's withers. She didn't mind at all.

When we reached our destination, Luke lifted the flap of the Poodle's ear and whispered, "I'll see you soon." I loved that. It looked as though his sessions would be a big success in more ways than one.

Faith and I were gone from our classroom for less than ten minutes. Upon our return, a woman I didn't recognize was standing beside my desk. She was thumbing through a stack of papers I'd left out. That was rude. I hoped she wasn't a parent of one of my students. Although they usually knew better than to show up without an appointment.

The woman looked about my age, and was dressed in jeans and a woolen peacoat, which she hadn't bothered to unbutton. Her hands were slender, with nails that were painted a shade of bright coral most women couldn't carry off. With her dark hair and olive-toned skin, the color looked stunning.

"Hello," I said, walking into the room. "Can I help you?"

She spun around. The frown on her face did nothing to enhance her good looks. "I certainly hope so. Are you Melanie Travis?"

"I am." I sent Faith to her bed. The woman barely flicked her a glance. "And you are?"

"Madison Penders. I've come to tell you to stay the hell out of my life."

Before replying, I stepped back and closed the classroom door. There was no need to broadcast this conversation. "How did you find me here?"

"You left me a message, remember? You said you worked at Howard Academy. Everybody in Greenwich knows about this place."

"That's true." I tried out a smile to see if it would soften Madison's expression. It didn't. "But visitors are supposed to check in at the office. You are not allowed to go strolling around the school without an escort."

"Nobody tried to stop me," she said, shrugging. "The doors in the back of the building are unlocked."

More's the pity, I thought.

If Madison had entered through the mansion's front door, she'd have run into Harriet. Then I'd have had some notice she was coming.

"I asked some lady where your classroom was, and she knew right away," Madison said. "I guess you must be pretty well known around here. Maybe because you're such a busybody."

Either that, or because I was a well-liked member of the faculty. Personally, I was hoping for the latter.

"Would you like to have a seat?" I asked.

She crossed her arms over her chest. "Why?"

"Since we're going to talk, I thought we might make ourselves comfortable."

"What makes you think we're going to talk?" Madison snapped. "I only came here to tell you to stop snooping around like some sort of cut-rate Nancy Drew. It's bad enough my father is dead. But your stupid questions are just making things worse."

"I'm sorry for your loss," I said.

"Really? Because it doesn't seem that way. You could try showing a little respect." Madison yanked out a chair and sat down. A minute earlier, I'd invited her to do so. Now I was no longer sure that was a good thing.

"It must have been hard losing your father so suddenly."

"It was. But his death wasn't nearly as bad as what

came before it. Having to watch the father I loved, the man who'd filled my childhood with laughter, fading further away from me every day. By the end, I hardly even knew who he was anymore."

"Dementia is a terrible impairment," I agreed. "I know it must have been difficult for you."

"Difficult." Madison snorted. "I've spent the last three years following my father around. Picking up after him. Cleaning up after him. Trying to talk to a man who barely remembers who I am. Having my needs become totally secondary to his. Like what I want to do with my life doesn't even matter anymore."

She stared up at me angrily. "Don't talk to me about *difficult*. Not unless you've ever been through something like that."

"I haven't," I said. "I've been lucky."

"Yeah, well, I wasn't."

Madison jumped back to her feet. She began to pace back and forth across the room. Faith and I both eyed her warily.

"And I don't need any of your fake sympathy either. You know what? My father's death was a mercy. Because the way he'd been living wasn't a real life. My father was a smart man once, one of the smartest I've ever met. Then his own brain betrayed him. Nobody should have to suffer through that."

"I agree," I said quietly. My sympathy had been well meant, but I wouldn't attempt to offer it again.

"All I want now is for my father to rest in peace," Madison growled. "But you keep stirring things up. I want you to leave us alone, understand? Why do you care who's to blame for what happened anyway?"

"Harriet Bloom is my friend," I said.

"So?"

"She's a suspect in your father's death."

"As she should be," Madison retorted. "If she hadn't given him those stupid marshmallow puffs, he would still be alive."

"That's not true," I said evenly. "There was nothing wrong with the puffs when Harriet delivered them to your father's house. Someone must have tampered with them after that."

Madison's face grew red. "Like who?" Her voice rose. "Like me? Is that what you're trying to say?"

"You tell me. I know Harriet is innocent—"

"Lady, you don't know squat." She turned and headed for the door. "You *think* Harriet is innocent. But that doesn't mean a damn thing."

"I'm listening," I said. "Tell me what I ought to know."

"Try listening to this. Butt. Out. You got it?"

Madison slammed the door behind her. Faith and I

both winced together. It was lucky the glass didn't break. I'd have hated to have to explain that to Mr. Hanover.

Madison was clearly harboring a ton of anger and resentment. Even before his death, the father she'd loved had already been lost to her. She'd called his death a mercy.

Now that he was gone, Madison had her life back. And maybe her dreams restored as well. That sounded like reason enough to commit murder to me.

That afternoon, I went to see someone who spends more time thinking about wrongdoers than anyone I know: Detective Raymond Young of the Greenwich PD. I wasn't taking any chances, so I called ahead and made an appointment. I figured there was always a chance he'd pretend to be out if I dropped by the station without warning.

The police station was in downtown Greenwich, so it wasn't far from Howard Academy. I found a shady parking spot a block away on Mason Street, and left Faith chewing on a rawhide bone I'd hidden in the glove compartment that morning.

Detective Young and I had a bit of history. Some of our previous interactions had been pretty prickly. Other times, we'd managed to collaborate in ways that had been productive for both of us. I was hoping for the latter experience this time. Based on the brief conversation we'd had at Howard Academy, however, I was also braced to encounter the former.

I checked in at the reception desk and took a seat. I'd barely had time to gather my thoughts before Detective Young appeared. His greeting was quite cordial. As I followed him to his office, I hoped that would set the tone for our conversation to come.

The previous time I'd come to discuss a case with the detective, I'd already knit together all the loose ends. This time, although I was sure the core of my narrative was sound, some of my reasoning was a little frayed around the edges. And there were loose threads dangling everywhere.

Maybe he could help with that, I thought hopefully.

Detective Young had left a straight-backed chair positioned in front of his desk. I took a seat without waiting to be asked. He closed the door and walked around behind his desk.

"I assume you're here about Harriet Bloom," he said.

"Yes. She didn't kill Ralph Penders."

"You still sound very sure of that."

"With good reason," I replied firmly.

I took off my jacket and hung it over the back of my chair. Like I was getting comfortable. Like I planned to be there awhile. I wasn't surprised that

Young noted the move. I suspected he didn't miss much.

He folded his hands together on his blotter and gave me his full attention. "Tell me why."

"I know Harriet. She's not the kind of person who would kill someone. And she's not an idiot. If Harriet had poisoned Ralph, she certainly wouldn't have left evidence sitting around that pointed in her direction."

Detective Young nodded.

I took that as an invitation to continue. "Even more important, she had no motive. Harriet had absolutely nothing to gain from Ralph's death."

"I gather the man was a nuisance around the neighborhood."

"Okay. But that gives everyone on her block the same motive. Plus, Harriet has a full-time job, so she's usually not home during the day. I could argue that since she's seldom there, she was less bothered by Ralph's behavior than most of her neighbors were."

The detective pursed his lips. He was thinking. I hoped that was a good sign.

"Also," I said. "Harriet didn't have the means to do it."

"She has admitted to baking the marshmallow puffs herself. And to delivering them to Ralph Penders."

"The puffs didn't kill him," I shot back. "The cyanide did. Harriet's a school administrator, where would she get cyanide?"

"You'd be amazed what can be found on the Internet these days," Detective Young said mildly.

I started to argue. He shook his head. I shut up.

"As it happens," he said. "I agree with almost everything you've said."

I stared at him. "Then why is Harriet still under investigation?"

"Principally because her attorney, Reginald Gordon, has blocked our access to Ms. Bloom. He's also restricted the availability of other household members. So we haven't been as successful at gathering information as we would have liked."

"What other household members?" I asked.

"Her sister, Bernadette Bloom, who assisted in the baking of the marshmallow puffs." He looked down and consulted his notes. "And a man named Hugh Grainger, who was at the Blooms' house when the delivery was made."

"Hugh is Bernadette's boyfriend," I said.

"So I was told. None of the three have been willing to speak with us, per Mr. Gordon's advice. So they remain persons of interest, and the investigation is ongoing."

"You must have other suspects," I pressed.

"That's not information I'm willing to divulge. But I know you, Ms. Travis. You wouldn't have come here simply to defend Ms. Bloom, especially not on such flimsy grounds as those you've offered. I suspect you have an alternate suspect you'd like me to consider."

"I do," I told him. "Madison Penders."

"Ralph Penders's daughter."

"Yes. As I'm sure you know, he was suffering from dementia."

Detective Young nodded.

"There wasn't enough money for him to be taken care of properly. Not in a nursing home, or with home care visits. As a result, Ralph was living on his own. Madison was supposed to be stopping in daily to see to his needs, but her visits had become less and less frequent. She was resentful of the demands he was making on her time."

"He was her father," Young said simply.

"Yes, but he was no longer the father she'd known and loved. That man had disappeared into a fog of lost memories. Instead, Madison was left tending to a belligerent old man, whom she felt she barely knew. And she hated it."

"She told you that?"

"Perhaps not in those exact words, but yes. And there's something else," I added.

"Go on."

"When I was talking to Bernadette a few days ago, she mentioned that she and Harriet had grown up in the house they live in. And that was good because they never could afford to buy it now. You know what property values are like in Greenwich."

"Of course."

"Ralph Penders had owned his home for more than twenty years. It's probably worth double what he paid for it. Even if the house was mortgaged, his heir would still collect a significant sum of money when it was sold." I looked at him across the desk. "I assume the family home was left to Madison?"

"It was," Young confirmed.

"Is she his only heir?"

"Aside from a few minor bequests to charity, yes." The detective paused to consider. "You believe that Madison Penders would be more capable of committing murder than Harriet Bloom would?"

"I think she had better reasons to," I told him. "And I don't think Madison would have thought of his death as murder. Actually, she called it a mercy."

"You make a compelling case for us to look into her further," Detective Young said.

"I do?" I sat up straighter in my chair. That had to be a good thing.

"There's just one problem."

Oh. I slumped back down. Why was there always a problem?

"On Friday evening, a week ago today, Ms. Bloom baked the batch of marshmallow puffs that Ralph Penders received. They were delivered to his home Saturday morning. He died that afternoon."

"Yes," I said. "So? Have you asked Madison where she was last weekend?"

"We have," he confirmed. "Ms. Penders was at a bachelorette party for a close friend. The party took place in Las Vegas, and five other women are willing to testify that she was there with them all weekend."

"Dammit," I said under my breath.

"My feelings precisely."

"Maybe someone helped her," I said. I wasn't willing to give up just yet. "Who else had access to Ralph's house?"

"The entire neighborhood, not to mention anyone else who happened to be passing by," Young replied with a frown. "I gather Mr. Penders wasn't vigilant about locking his doors."

Another *dammit* felt called for. Instead, I said, "So what do we do now?"

The detective stopped just short of rolling his eyes. "Now I continue my investigation, and you go home and prepare to enjoy your Halloween."

Faith was delighted to see me when I got back to the car. She dropped the rawhide bone and launched herself into my arms. Good thing the open door was behind me, because she nearly knocked me over.

"That didn't help at all," I told her.

Faith didn't care. She was just happy I'd returned. *Thank God for dogs,* I thought.

Chapter
Fifteen

Detective Young had shot down my best theory pretty spectacularly. As he'd said, there was nothing for me to do now but go home and get ready for Halloween. The Howard Academy party was just a few hours away. And I still had a costume to make.

Sam knew I'd been crazy busy all week. I hadn't even questioned why he'd volunteered to pick up Kev at school earlier. If I was really lucky, maybe he had a plan.

If not, I was hoping that a black turtleneck, a pair of jeans, and an iPhone would do the trick.

Faith and I walked into the house and didn't get mobbed by Standard Poodles. That was different. The rooms around us were quiet and still.

Faith and I looked at each other. Then her ears pricked. Her nose pointed toward the kitchen and off she went. All I had to do was follow.

The kitchen was empty too. Then I realized I was

wrong about where the Standard Poodle was heading. Faith stopped beside the back door, dancing eagerly on her toes. She couldn't figure out what was taking me so long to get it.

Of course. Everybody was outside.

As soon as I opened the door, I could hear the shrieks of laughter too. Tar and Augie were racing around the perimeter of the big, fenced-in yard. Eve and Raven were running in pursuit.

Kevin and Bud were out in the grass, wrestling over something that both were holding on to. When Bud suddenly let go, Kev flew backward and landed on his butt. That was Bud's cue to pounce on top of him. More shrieking ensued.

Sam was standing on the deck, watching the mayhem unfold. Even from the back, he looked good.

I walked up behind him and slipped my arms around his waist. Sam covered my hands with his own and pulled me closer. Maybe Faith's and my arrival hadn't been as stealthy as I'd thought.

"What's going on?" I stood on my toes to peer over Sam's shoulder.

"Kev's giving his Halloween costume a trial run."

Abruptly Kevin rolled away from Bud and jumped up. He came running toward us. "Ahoy, mateys!" he cried.

He had on a striped, long-sleeved T-shirt and black pants. The red sash around his waist looked like something from the bottom of my scarf drawer. A home-made eye patch covered one of Kev's eyes. And he was gleefully brandishing a rubber sword.

So that was what he and Bud had been tussling over. No wonder Kev had wanted it back. What five-year-old boy wouldn't want to have a pirate's cutlass to slash through the air? The costume was perfect.

"I love you," I whispered in Sam's ear.

"I know," he replied.

I punched him in the shoulder.

"What?" Sam was all innocence. "Would it have been better if I'd said, 'You should'?"

"Not much," I agreed. "Good work with the costume."

"Time was passing," he mentioned. "Someone had to do something."

A sassy retort rose to mind, but I tamped it back down. Frankly, I was just happy he'd noticed.

When Davey's bus dropped him off an hour later, Kev was still wearing his costume. Davey made an appropriately large fuss over it. Then the two of them went out to play pirates in the tree house.

"Don't let Kev make Bud walk the plank," I warned Davey.

"Give me some credit. I'm almost an adult."

He couldn't even drive yet. That wasn't almost an adult to me.

Still, it was old enough that Davey hadn't been

pressed into accompanying us to the HA Halloween party. Instead he'd be spending his Friday evening with friends, no costumes involved. The following night, he and I would stay home to hand out candy to trick-or-treaters, while Sam squired Kevin around the neighborhood.

"I can't believe I let you rope me into wearing matching costumes," Sam grumbled later that evening as we were getting ready to go.

"I think you look great," I said with a grin. "The black mustache looks a little funny with your blond hair, but other than that . . ."

Sam and I were going to the party dressed as Gomez and Morticia Addams. I was wearing a slinky black dress with a push-up bra and a long black wig. Sam had on a striped suit and a bow tie. He was carrying a prop cigar.

The costumes had been easy to put together, plus they'd keep us warm on the brisk October night. I knew Cheryl was dressing up as Wonder Woman. I figured she'd probably regret that later.

Halloween was a hugely popular holiday at Howard Academy. Children, parents, and teachers were all invited to the party, and costumes put everyone in a festive mood. There were booths where kids could bob for apples, bowl with pumpkins, and turn their parents into mummies with a toilet paper wrap. The highlight of the event was an exuberant costume parade. Everyone was invited to take part, and winners were declared in numerous categories.

We arrived at Howard Academy a little early, but when we turned in the long driveway, there were already cars ahead of us heading up the hill to the school. The mansion was ablaze with lights, illuminating an approach that was now lined with fake gravestones and leering skeletons. Long strands of cotton batting hung from the tree branches like cobwebs, fluttering eerily in the evening breeze. Kev stared out the car window with his mouth open.

The decorations were wonderful, and the old mansion looked suitably spooky. Harriet and Cheryl must have been busy all afternoon.

I directed Sam around the back of the new building. Mr. Hanover would be greeting guests at the mansion's front door, but if we parked in the rear, we could go directly to the auditorium where the party was being held.

"I feel like an idiot," Sam muttered as we got out of the SUV.

"It's Halloween," I told him. "You're supposed to look silly."

He gazed around the parking lot. In the semidarkness, it was hard to tell what other people were wearing. I'd attended the holiday party many times before. But this was Kevin's first year as a student at Howard Academy, so it was Sam's first appearance.

"Are you *sure* that parents are supposed to get dressed up too?"

"Positive. Last year, one father came as Julius Caesar and his wife was Cleopatra. They came rolling in on a motorized sedan chair."

"You're kidding." He stared at me.

"I wish. Another man came as bacon. His wife was a fried egg."

Sam laughed in spite of himself. "That's terrible."

"I know, it was. But see? You'll be fine. Compared to that, you look almost normal."

Kevin had stepped away from the car. He was slashing at a nearby bush with his rubber cutlass. His eye patch was on crooked. It probably wouldn't last the night, but I reached down and fixed it anyway.

Sam leaned over to peer in the SUV's side mirror. "I look like Groucho Marx."

"Not when you're standing next to me," I pointed out. "Then people will get it."

"You make a beautiful Morticia." Sam grinned. "I like the wig." His gaze dropped to my chest. "And whatever you put on underneath that dress."

"Hold that thought," I told him as I grabbed Kev's hand. "First we have a party to attend."

The school auditorium had been transformed. It no

longer looked like a bright, spacious meeting place. Instead, dim lighting now made the large room feel surprisingly close. Bats and spiders hung from the ceiling. A decrepit-looking haunted house sagged against some folded bleachers. Skeletons danced on the empty stage. An invisible projector sent ghostly images flying over the walls. Carved pumpkins, lit with flickering candles, decorated most surfaces. As we walked past an innocent-looking screen, a witch popped out from behind it and greeted us with a mad cackle.

Kev's small hand trembled within mine. He cradled his sword close to his side. I stopped walking and squatted down to look him in the eye.

"You doing okay, buddy?"

He nodded.

"You know this is all just make-believe, right?"

Another nod.

"It's supposed to be spooky, but not really scary," I told him. "Nothing here can hurt you. Dad and I would never let anything bad happen."

Kevin lifted his other hand in a show of bravado. "And I have my cutlass!"

"If you see any real ghosts, you have my permission to knock them down," Sam said, joining the conversation.

"Aye, aye, Captain!" Kev cried. Just that quickly, he was feeling better.

His gaze lit on a booth where kids from his class

were tossing beanbags into a barrel painted to look like a giant pumpkin. His hand dropped mine, then grabbed Sam's. He gestured with his sword. "Can we go play too?"

"Sure, that's why we're here," Sam replied, then turned to me. "Why don't you go mingle and do teacher stuff. We'll catch up with you later."

"Sounds good. There are plenty of refreshments if you guys get hungry or thirsty."

"Don't worry about us," Sam said. Kev was already tugging him away. "We'll find our way around."

I set out to find Cheryl and Harriet. Even though the party was in progress, I knew there would still be things that needed to be done. Maybe I could help.

I saw the two women conferring with each other near the food tables. That was handy. On my way past, I paused to peruse the offerings. There was plenty of real food, but it was the desserts that drew my attention.

There were cookies shaped and iced to look like pumpkins and black cats. The cupcakes were topped with decorative spiderwebs. And the punch came in two colors: deep purple and orange. Despite those options, the table still looked as though it was missing something. And it was. A tray of Harriet's delicious marshmallow puffs.

Cheryl lifted a hand and waved me over. I grabbed

a cookie and went to join them. Harriet was resplendent in an elaborate witch's costume that would have passed muster in a production of *Wicked*. Wearing high boots and a long cape, Cheryl made a terrific Wonder Woman. A gold diadem on her forehead was the crowning touch.

Cheryl looked me up and down. "Morticia Addams, right?"

"Yes, and my husband, Sam, is Gomez. So whatever you do, don't ask him if he's supposed to be Groucho Marx."

We laughed together.

"Did Bernadette come with you?" I asked Harriet.

"No, I told her family members were welcome, but Bernie opted for a quiet night at home." She gazed around the crowded room. "And considering the crush this is turning into, I don't blame her one bit."

"This place looks amazing," I said. "Kids are lined up at all the game booths, and everything on the buffet table is totally tempting. I have no idea how you're making those skeletons dance, but I absolutely love it. It's a good thing I bowed out when I did, because the two of you have done a terrific job."

"Thank you, but we can't take all the credit," Harriet replied. "Cheryl and I had plenty of assistance pulling everything together. The grounds crew assembled the haunted house and the booths. The boys' soccer team helped put up the decorations. And the kitchen staff worked overtime to supply most of the food."

"I came over to see if you needed anything, but now I just feel redundant," I said with a smile.

"Yikes." Cheryl grimaced. "It looks like there's an issue with the apple bobbing. I'll just go take care of that . . ." She flung her cape back over her shoulder and hurried away.

"Wonder Woman indeed," Harriet said fondly. "I'm glad this party gave me the opportunity to get to know Cheryl better. She's a great addition to the Howard Academy family."

I agreed. But now that she'd left us, I took the chance to bring Harriet up to date on what I'd been doing since we'd last compared notes.

"I talked to Detective Young earlier today," I told her.

"You did?" Harriet looked surprised. And that surprised me.

"Mr. Hanover didn't tell you that he'd asked me to do so?"

"No," she replied unhappily. "I'm afraid my relationship with the headmaster is a bit strained at the moment."

I reached over and gave her arm a squeeze. "That won't last. As soon as this mess is cleared up, everything will go back to normal."

"I wish I were as sure of that as you are." Harriet stopped and sighed. "I offered to make new batches of marshmallow puffs for the party. I said I would bake them in the kitchen here at HA, under Mrs. Plimpton's direct supervision. And that they wouldn't be out of our sight until we put them out on the table. Mr. Hanover still didn't think that was a wise idea."

"What a shame," I commiserated with her. "Your marshmallow puffs are always the highlight of the occasion. The buffet table looks empty without them. But you'll be happy to hear that I have some good news."

"Well, that's a relief." Harriet mustered a smile. "I was afraid this party was going to be all gloom and doom. Lay it on me."

"Detective Young doesn't believe that you were responsible for Ralph's death."

Her smile brightened. "Does that mean I'm no longer a suspect?"

"Not exactly," I admitted. "But at least now you have the detective on your side. I think you should take your lawyer and go have a conversation with him. One where you cooperate and answer his questions."

"That's probably not a bad idea. Does he have other suspects now?"

"Unfortunately, Detective Young wasn't willing to

tell me that. I suggested he look into Madison Penders. She sneaked in the back door of the new building and showed up in my classroom this morning."

"She did?" Harriet frowned at the breach of school protocol. "What did she want?"

"Madison told me to back off and stop asking questions. She didn't seem very upset about her father's death. She said it was a mercy that he was gone."

"Did you relay all that to Detective Young?"

"I did, but it didn't help. Because then he told me that Madison was in Las Vegas with friends when Ralph died."

We both pondered that briefly.

"Maybe she was smart enough to set herself up with a good alibi," Harriet mused aloud. "I'm not convinced that lets her off the hook. What if she had an accomplice? Someone who was willing to doctor the marshmallow puffs after she was gone."

"I like the way your mind works," I said. "I was thinking the very same thing earlier. But we need to figure out who her helper could have been."

Harriet gave me a nudge. "You're supposed to be the experienced sleuth in this partnership. How come you don't have the answer already?"

I knew she was kidding, but I defended myself anyway. "I never met the woman before today. I hardly know anything about her."

"Nor do I," Harriet admitted. "Madison moved out of her father's house years ago. Her personal life is a complete mystery to me. The only thing I do know is that she's a very angry young woman. Madison feels as though life hasn't dealt her a fair hand. So maybe the idea of a mercy killing isn't as far-fetched as it sounds."

There was a sudden commotion near the auditorium's double-door entrance. We both turned to look. A large chariot was trying to maneuver its way into the room.

"Oh Lord," Harriet groaned. "Not the Petersons again. Darn that man's obsession with ancient Rome. I'd better go see what I can do to manage things before they get out of hand. Can we finish this conversation later?"

"Absolutely," I said, stifling a laugh. I was glad the chariot and its occupants weren't my problem. "One last thing to think about before you go."

"Yes?" She was anxious to be on her way.

"It could be that battering your mailbox wasn't enough of a revenge for Madison," I said. "And that's why she framed you for her father's murder."

Chapter Sixteen

I spent the next half hour browsing around the party. Between checking out the booths, praising children's costumes, and giving directions to the buffet and the bathrooms, there was plenty to keep me busy. I was on my way back to the dessert table to nab a cupcake when a small blond tiger stepped into my path.

I squinted down at the striped mask that covered half his face. "Luke, is that you?"

"Rraaarr!" The boy put so much effort into the roar that the ears on top of his head waggled back and forth.

I stepped back in mock horror. "Wow, I'm impressed. You look very fierce."

"That was the point." A woman standing behind him was dressed as a Supreme Court justice. More Sandra Day O'Connor than RBG. "I'm Beverly Chism, Luke's mother. You're Melanie Travis, right?"

"That's right. It's a pleasure to meet you." Compared to Beverly's demure outfit, my costume suddenly felt a little low-cut and a lot too tight. Maybe I should have considered the fact that I'd be talking to parents tonight when I'd chosen my attire.

Then Beverly smiled and held out her hand. "Great costume. Morticia?"

I nodded as we shook hands.

"Good for you. I'd wear something like that if I could fit into it. I wanted to talk to you about Luke."

"Of course." That was a relief. "He and I have just started working together. I'm delighted to have him in my classroom."

"And he's thrilled to be there," Beverly told me. "Especially because of your lovely Standard Poodle, Faith. He hasn't stopped talking about her since he met her."

"Faith's a great dog. All the kids love her." I paused, then added, because I was curious, "But most of them don't know right away that she's a Standard Poodle."

"Yes, I'd imagine they wouldn't." Beverly laughed. "But that's precisely the reason that Luke was so drawn to her. We had a Standard Poodle named Molly for many years. She was black, just like yours. Luke had Molly for his entire life, until she passed away last summer. She was a wonderful dog, and he was heartbroken."

"I'm sorry," I said. "I know how difficult it is to lose a dog who's a member of your family."

"Molly was so special, I knew we'd never be able to replace her. In fact, I was hesitant to even try. I didn't want to get another dog and have Luke be disappointed that it wasn't the same. But then he walked into your classroom this morning and saw Faith . . ."

Beverly's eyes were moist. Another minute of this and I'd be sniffling too.

"Luke took one look at your Standard Poodle and fell head over heels in love." Beverly raised her hands and placed them together as if in prayer. "So I'm hoping that you can help me. The woman we got Molly from is no longer breeding, but maybe if you could tell me where Faith came from . . . ?"

"I can do better than that," I told her. "I can introduce you. Faith's breeder is my Aunt Peg. She lives right here in Greenwich. She doesn't have many litters anymore, but she knows everyone in the Poodle world. I'm sure she can find you a black Standard Poodle puppy, if you want her to."

"We do!" Luke cried. He'd been listening to our conversation. Now he was staring at me, wide-eyed. "Will my puppy grow up to look like Faith?"

"Just like her," I told him. "And she'll have the same terrific temperament. Aunt Peg will make sure she's had all her genetic testing too."

Unexpectedly, Beverly threw her arms around me.

Then Luke jumped in and wrapped his arms around my waist from the other side. It was an odd feeling being hugged by a tiger and a Supreme Court justice at the same time.

"Thank you so much," Beverly cried. "That would be absolutely wonderful, wouldn't it, Luke?"

The small boy bobbed his head up and down several times to make sure I got the message.

"I'll talk to Aunt Peg tomorrow and be in touch," I said.

"Perfect." Beverly was beaming as she took Luke's hand. "We'll be waiting to hear from you."

I watched the two of them walk away. Luke was skipping with excitement. Beverly reached down and ruffled her son's hair. They shared a happy smile. After the frustrations I'd experienced on Harriet's behalf, it felt great to be able to do something good for someone.

"Is everything all right, Ms. Travis?"

I spun around in place. I hadn't heard Mr. Hanover approach. Obviously, he'd been watching us.

"Yes, fine," I said. "Maybe perfect."

"Perfect?" He looked startled. Then pleased. "Well done, then. Who was the woman with whom you were speaking?"

"Beverly Chism. Her son, Luke, is in first grade. Cheryl Feeney's class."

"Ah, yes. The family is new this year. I shall have

to go and introduce myself." He looked at me specula-tively. "Something you said made them very happy."

"Luke fell in love with Faith. They'd recently lost their own Poodle and I offered to find them another to replace her."

"I see. I expect Peg might be able to help with that?"

Of course he knew Aunt Peg. She wasn't just a Howard Academy alumna, she was also a generous donor.

"I'm sure she can."

"Very well, then. Carry on."

"Pip-pip and tallyho," I said under my breath as he walked away. Mr. Hanover often had that effect on me.

An announcement came over the loudspeaker. The costume parade was about to begin. Everyone who intended to take part was invited to assemble near the stage. I knew Kevin wanted to be in the parade. Sam and I were planning to walk with him. Now all I had to do was find them in this crowd.

I was up on my toes, gazing around the room, when someone jostled me from behind. Nearly everyone was on the move now. All were heading in the direction of either the stage or the parade route in the center of the room. I was the only one who was standing still.

"Sorry," said a voice that sounded almost familiar. "I should be more careful."

I turned around and looked at him. The man who'd

knocked into me was wearing a close-fitting devil costume. There were horns on his head, and a dark cape swirled around his shoulders. Unlike most of the adults at the party, he had on a mask. It covered the upper half of his face.

"No problem." I stared at him curiously as people continued to move past us. "I was in your way."

He tipped his head to one side and smiled. "Don't you recognize me?"

"No, I'm afraid I don't. Should I?"

He pulled down the mask briefly, then let it slip back into place. I'd expected to see a school parent. Instead, the man was Bernadette's friend, Hugh Grainger. What was he doing here?

"You look surprised to see me." His voice was low and silky smooth.

"I am. I didn't expect you to be here."

Hugh shrugged. "I hate to miss a party. I came with Bernie."

"You did?" I frowned. "I thought she wasn't coming tonight."

"She changed her mind. Come on." He folded his fingers over my arm. "I know where she is. I'll show you."

"That's all right, I can see her later." I tried to pull my arm away. Hugh didn't let go. "I'm going over to the costume parade now."

"No," said Hugh. "I don't think you are."

A shiver slipped up the back of my neck. In the

brief time that he and I had been talking, the area of the room where we were standing had emptied out. Even the booths had shut down for the parade.

Loud music was now blasting through speakers near the ceiling. People were crowded together in the center of the auditorium, clapping and cheering. The parade must be starting. Everyone was looking in the opposite direction. Even if someone did glance our way, Hugh and I would be barely visible in the shadows at the perimeter of the room.

With all that noise, no one would hear me if I called for help.

"Let go of me," I said through gritted teeth.

"No." He smiled again, a distinctly feral look, as if he knew something I didn't. "You and I are going to take a little walk."

Not if I can help it, I thought. "Where are we going?"

"The haunted house should be deserted now. I think we'll step inside."

I planted my feet. If Hugh intended to make me move, he was going to have to drag me.

"Why?" I asked, still stalling.

"Good question," he snapped. "Why couldn't you leave things alone?"

"What things?"

Hugh squeezed my arm harder and I winced. "Don't

play dumb, Melanie Travis. Whatever other annoying things you are, you're not stupid."

"This is about Ralph Penders," I said.

Hugh's next yank pulled me off my feet. The Morticia dress, wound tightly around my legs, was hampering my ability to resist. Now I was going with him, whether I wanted to or not.

"Did you kill him?" I asked.

Hugh glared down at me. "Of course not."

"Do you know who did?"

"We both know the answer to that. It was his daughter, Madison. She hated that life was passing her by while she was stuck caring for a sick old man—a father who barely remembered who she was. His death was best for both of them."

Hugh had told me that he'd never met Madison. So it was interesting that he now claimed to know so much about her feelings. And her actions. Not to mention that he'd come to her defense.

Abruptly I looked at him in a new light. Hugh was clearly a liar. And probably an opportunist. And then there was Madison, who'd been out of town when her father died. She'd needed someone else to do her dirty work for her.

Detective Young had mentioned that Hugh was there when Ralph's marshmallow puffs were delivered. Why hadn't I picked up on that earlier? Suddenly it was looking as though Bernadette's annoying beau must have been Madison's accomplice all along.

Dammit, I thought. Harriet and I had been *so close*. We'd had everything figured out except the one thing we needed most—a name. I hoped I lived long enough to share Hugh's with Detective Young.

He and I had almost reached the haunted house. The creaky structure looked suitably spooky. Its walls tilted. Its windows were blacked out. Once we were inside, Hugh could do anything he wanted. No one would be able to see or hear us.

I had to keep stalling—and hope that someone would realize I was missing and come looking for me.

"You and Madison must be close," I said.

Hugh didn't reply.

"I thought you were with Bernadette."

He hiked my arm upward and pain shot through my shoulder. "Bernie was . . . convenient."

I grimaced and kept walking. "I don't understand."

"Bernie was useful. She was a means to get to Harriet. Through her job, that damn woman probably has more influential connections than anyone in Greenwich." He scowled. "Not that they ever did me any good."

I was shocked by his answer. "You mean at Howard Academy?"

"Of course that's what I mean," Hugh snapped.

"Harriet could have introduced me to important people. She was supposed to be my conduit to all these
rich parents."

The gallantry and charm with which Hugh had
treated Bernadette was nowhere in evidence now. I
was seeing a whole new side of him. One I hadn't
even suspected.

"All I needed was an entrée," he said. "I'd have
worked things out myself from there. Except that
Harriet wouldn't cooperate."

"That Harriet," I replied. "She's a bitch."

"Tell me about it," Hugh muttered. "I spent all
that time cultivating Bernie, and for what? *Nothing.*
Then one day when I was at her house, I met Ralph.
What a pathetic old man he was. But when I took
him back where he belonged, I met Madison. That's
when a new picture began to emerge."

He meant a new score to pursue, I realized. Bernie
didn't offer him enough. Harriet wasn't cooperating
with his plans. And there was unhappy, impression-
able, Madison. Ralph's only child, she'd be heir to his
possessions, including that nice piece of real estate.

"Madison and I hit it off right away," Hugh said.

Of course they had. Hugh would have made sure
of that. Just like he'd convinced Bernadette that he
was in love with her.

"And then . . . you know. It was a kindness what
happened to the old guy."

"A kindness." I snorted. "You killed him."

Hugh shrugged. "It was his time to go."

We'd reached the haunted house. Like everything else in the vicinity, the attraction was deserted. It wasn't cold inside the room, but I'd begun to shiver.

Hugh was still grasping my arm. He must have felt me shudder. "I didn't mean for things to turn out this way," he said, making an effort to sound remorseful.

I wasn't buying it. To me, he just looked like the Devil.

"I didn't either," I muttered.

"Bernie told me you'd been figuring things out. And that you were going to talk to the police. I can't allow that. I'm not going to let you screw this up for me." His hand reached around inside his cape. "Here, I brought you something."

Hugh held out the offering in his palm. My eyes widened. It was one of Harriet's marshmallow puffs.

"Where did you get that?"

"I picked it up at the food table." He waved vaguely in the direction of the buffet. "I thought you might want something to snack on while we finish our conversation."

Yeah, right. I wasn't about to touch that thing. Despite what Hugh had said earlier, he must have been hoping I was thick as a brick.

"I'm not hungry," I said. "You can have it."

"No, it's for you." He thrust the puff at my face. "Eat it."

I clamped my lips shut. I'd bite him before I'd let him force that poisoned puff down my throat.

Hugh lifted my hand and placed the sticky treat in my palm. "Go on, take a bite."

Obediently I curled my fingers around the marshmallow puff. I raised my hand toward my mouth. A grim smile played around the edges of Hugh's lips. Sure that he was getting what he wanted, he relaxed fractionally.

So when my clenched fist shot upward and caught him beneath the chin, he never saw it coming. Hugh's head flew up. His mouth snapped shut. He staggered backward, trying to find his balance.

Even so, Hugh didn't release his hold on my arm. That meant I was dragged along with him. Reaching down with sticky fingers, I frantically tried to pry myself free.

Hugh stumbled, then found his feet again. A trickle of blood dribbled from his mouth. He'd probably bitten his tongue. The expression on his face was murderous.

I'd hurt him, but I hadn't done enough to stop him. Now Hugh would make sure I didn't get a second chance.

Then I saw something moving in the shadows behind him. For a moment, I thought I must be imagining things—because it looked as though a large pumpkin was coming toward us. I blinked and looked again.

Hugh heard something too. He started to turn around, but he wasn't fast enough. The orange orb lifted high in the air, then came crashing down on his head. The pumpkin split in half with a loud crack. Its guts went flying everywhere.

Hugh dropped to the floor like a rock. This time, he didn't get up.

Harriet was standing behind him. In her black witch's costume, she'd blended into the dark background. But even in the gloom, I could see her face. She was smiling with satisfaction.

"Bitch indeed," she said.

Chapter
Seventeen

I was pretty sure this night would go down in the annals of Howard Academy as the time I'd ruined the school Halloween party. Even though I couldn't see any way this whole mess had been my fault.

Amazingly, the parade continued, uninterrupted, while Harriet pulled out her phone and called 911. Music was still playing. Parents and kids were laughing and dancing, and showing off their costumes.

As I was tying Hugh's hands with a length of rope I'd found in the haunted house, Cheryl announced the winners of the costume contest, which led to more celebration. A good time was being had by all. Except, of course, for Hugh, who regained consciousness with an angry snarl on his face.

By the time the police arrived, Mr. Hanover had been notified of the events that had unfolded virtually behind his back. Thankfully, the other partygoers remained blissfully unaware of the crisis that had been so narrowly avoided. Even the uniformed officers who'd responded to Harriet's call looked like they were in costume.

So it was all good, right?

Well, not entirely.

Harriet and I both still had a lot of questions to answer. And Hugh immediately got busy denying everything we said. He told the two officers he'd only come to the Halloween party to enjoy himself, and had no idea why two crazy women had attacked him with a pumpkin.

The fact that Hugh was dressed as the Devil probably didn't bolster his credibility. I also made one of the officers scrape that sticky marshmallow puff up off the floor and put it in an evidence bag. Once the lab had a chance to test it, the results went a long way toward supporting Harriet's and my story.

I had one last interview with Detective Young. Harriet had officially been cleared of suspicion in the death of Ralph Penders. But there was still one question remaining.

"Did Hugh kill Ralph on his own?" I asked. "Or did he and Madison act together?"

"We're still not entirely clear on that," he admitted. "Since their arrests, the two of them have turned on each other. Ms. Penders says she never would have left town if she'd known what Mr. Grainger had in mind. He says that getting rid of her father was all her idea, and he was only following her instructions."

Luckily for me, I didn't have to figure out who was telling the truth and who wasn't. Ralph's killers had been caught. Now it was up to the police, the lawyers, and the judicial system to sort out the rest. As long as Harriet was in the clear, and her job at Howard Academy was once again secure, I was happy with the outcome.

The same couldn't be said for Harriet's sister, Bernadette. The poor woman had thought she was in love with Hugh. Finding out that she'd fallen for a con man, who was only cultivating her for her sister's connections, had come as a bitter blow.

"She's feeling pretty low," Harriet told me. "But Bernie's resilient. She'll bounce back. I put a dating app on her phone. She told me she wasn't interested, but I caught her sneaking a look. 'Just to see what's out there."

Oh Lord, I thought. *That could be out of the frying pan and into the fire.* At least this time, Harriet had promised to keep a closer eye on her sister's amorous adventures.

After all the turmoil leading up to it, Halloween itself went off without a hitch. Sam escorted a swashbuckling Kev around the neighborhood. Davey liked his own costume idea so much that he dressed up as Steve Jobs to help me hand out candy to trick-or-treaters. Bud and the Standard Poodles lined up in the front hall and greeted each new arrival with wagging tails and doggy grins. It was just the kind of diversion we all needed.

The following week, Beverly and Luke Chism met with Aunt Peg. I had told her that Luke was a quiet child, who was apt to be reserved in unfamiliar company, and that he'd recently lost his own beloved Standard Poodle. Aunt Peg had pondered that for a minute as she gazed at her own canine crew. Then, without sharing her thoughts with me, she'd simply promised to be on her best behavior.

Aunt Peg and I were waiting at her house when the Chisms arrived. She opened her front door and her five black Poodles went flying down the front steps. Regular visitors were accustomed to that boisterous greeting. I hoped Beverly and Luke wouldn't mind.

Luke slowly got out of the car. The Poodles were leaping and playing in the front yard. Seeing him, they raced in his direction as a group, then skidded to a stop. Luke gazed around in wonder. Five faces, all similar to his Molly, gazed back at him.

The dogs seemed to sense his reticence. They waited until Luke was ready before completing their approach. He held out his hands. One by one, the Poodles stepped forward to check him out. His fingers lightly grazed the topknot of Aunt Peg's senior dog, whose muzzle was gray with age.

"That's Beau," Aunt Peg told him. "He's thirteen. And very much the king of all he surveys. He likes you, and that means I do too."

Luke offered her a shy smile, which Aunt Peg returned in spades. I don't know why I'd ever worried.

Beverly came around the front of the car and I introduced everyone. Then we went inside to sit down and talk Poodles. The dogs, of course, came with us. While the three adults got comfortable on couches and chairs, Luke joined the Standard Poodles on the floor.

Beverly told Aunt Peg all about the wonderful life Molly had enjoyed with her family. She volunteered information about their fenced yard, mobile groomer, and veterinary references. She spoke about how Luke was mourning the loss of his dog, and said she would be grateful if Aunt Peg could help them find them a suitable puppy. Beverly hoped it wouldn't take too long.

Luke, meanwhile, had gathered the Poodles in a circle around him. The group appeared to be engaged in their own private conversation.

Each time his hand touched a different Poodle, Aunt Peg would quietly supply the dog's name. Luke would repeat it, then pause to look for a response. He grinned as each Poodle licked his fingers or placed its head in his lap.

"That's Hope," I told him when the pretty bitch took her turn. "She's Faith's sister."

"She looks like Faith," Luke replied. "They have the same eyes."

They did, indeed. Although most people didn't notice such a small detail upon first acquaintance. I saw Aunt Peg nod approvingly.

A dainty black bitch stepped to the front of the group. She sniffed Luke's hand, then his shoulder. Then she leaned forward and nudged his chin. When the boy laughed, she pushed Hope aside and carefully lay down on top of Luke's crossed legs. She was a big Poodle, so it took some maneuvering to get them both comfortable.

Luke leaned down—it wasn't very far—and gave her a hug. He buried his face in her dense hair.

"Willow's a very good judge of character," Aunt Peg said. "She doesn't make herself at home in just anybody's lap."

"I'm glad she chose mine," Luke said happily, his arms still looped around the Poodle's neck.

"Your Poodles are wonderful." Beverly smiled down at her son. "My husband and I would be thrilled to have one just like them for Luke. Please say you'll help us find a breeder. Melanie told me you have many connections in the Poodle world. I'd be happy to supply more references, or anything else you need."

"Oh, I think I'll be able to come up with a good idea or two." Aunt Peg's eyes were twinkling. She looked very pleased with herself.

I wondered what she was up to now.

"I just have one question," Aunt Peg said. "Do you have your heart set on a puppy?"

Beverly considered briefly, then shook her head. "No, an adult Poodle would be fine too." She looked at her son. "Right, Luke?"

He nodded. He was still holding Willow close.

"Are you thinking about a dog from a rescue situation?" Beverly asked. "Maybe one that didn't work out for someone else?"

"Not exactly," Aunt Peg told her. "At one time, I was a very active Standard Poodle breeder and exhibitor. Now, however, I spend much of my time judging dog shows. It's a job that demands quite a bit of travel, so I've cut back on the number of dogs I keep at home."

My gaze sharpened. All at once, I suspected I knew what she was going to say next.

Beverly was listening, waiting for Aunt Peg to make her point. Luke had lifted the flap of Willow's ear. He was confiding a secret to her.

"As you know, Poodles are people dogs. More than anything, they want to be by their person's side.

So the fact that I'm often away from home isn't a perfect situation. For me, or for them." Aunt Peg looked down at the Poodles spread out on the floor around us.

"If you would be open to the idea, I would consider placing one of my Poodles with you," she continued. "Willow would thrive in a home where she was the only dog. Especially one where there was a young boy who wanted to devote all his attention to her."

I heard a gasp. It came from Luke. His head swiveled around. He looked up at his mother imploringly. "Can we, Mom? Can we?"

Beverly stared at Aunt Peg. She was surprised too. "Are you sure? It seems like almost too much to ask."

"I'm quite sure." Aunt Peg smiled. "I wouldn't make an offer like this lightly. But I think it could work out well for all of us. Especially Willow, who would love to have a child like Luke to play with every day."

"I don't know quite what to say," Beverly sputtered.

"Say yes!" Luke cried. "Please, Mommy."

"Yes," she agreed happily. "Yes, of course. Luke and I would be delighted to take you up on your offer."

"Good, then we'll start with a trial period . . ."

I left when Aunt Peg began outlining how they would proceed. They could work out the details among themselves. As usual, Aunt Peg had come up with a solution that was both unexpected and at the same time utterly perfect.

I got in the Volvo and went home to my family. And my Poodles. And a big pile of leftover Halloween candy. Harriet had even stopped by to drop off a batch of marshmallow puffs she'd made especially for me. I couldn't wait to dig in.

After the week I'd had, I deserved a serious sugar rush.

HARRIET BLOOM'S MARSHMALLOW PUFFS

Harriet's secret recipe is easy to make and delicious to eat. These sweet treats will stick to your fingers and are best served chilled. The perfect indulgence for an autumn afternoon.

Ingredients:

Base
    2 ounces unsweetened chocolate
    6 tbsps (¾ stick) butter
    1 cup sugar
    2 small eggs
    ½ tsp vanilla
    ½ cup flour

Toppings
    1 package mini marshmallows
    4 ounces semisweet chocolate chips
    1-2 tbsps milk

Preheat oven to 350 degrees. Grease or spray a 9- x 13-inch baking pan.

Microwave unsweetened chocolate and butter in a microwave-safe bowl for 45–60 seconds, then stir until the chocolate is completely melted. Add the remaining base ingredients, mixing together thoroughly as you go along. The batter will be thick. Take care to spread it evenly in the baking pan.

Bake for 12–13 minutes until a toothpick inserted in the middle comes out clean. Remove pan from oven and add a generous topping of mini marshmallows. (I throw on the whole bag.) Return to the oven for 4–5 minutes until the marshmallows melt together and begin to turn golden. Remove from oven and set aside to cool.

Put the semisweet chocolate chips in a microwave-safe bowl. Melt in the microwave, stirring frequently (about 1 minute). If the chocolate is too thick, stir in 1-2 tbsps of milk to thin. Drizzle the chocolate topping over the marshmallows.

Chill thoroughly and enjoy.